The AMAZON PAPERS

Beverly Keller

BROWNDEER PRESS

HARCOURT BRACE & COMPANY

San Diego   New York   London

Requests for permission to make copies
of any part of the work should be mailed to:
Permissions Department, Harcourt Brace & Company,
6277 Sea Harbor Drive, Orlando, Florida 32887-6777.

Browndeer Press is a registered trademark
of Harcourt Brace & Company.

Library of Congress Cataloging-in-Publication Data
Keller, Beverly.
The Amazon papers/Beverly Keller.
p. cm.
"Browndeer Press."
Summary: Fifteen-year-old Iris gets into hilarious trouble
when her mother goes on vacation and leaves her alone.
ISBN 0-15-201345-8   ISBN 0-15-201346-6 (pbk.)
[1. Humorous stories.] I. Title.
PZ7.K2813Am   1996
[Fic]—dc20   96-7756

Text set in Columbus
Designed by Linda Lockowitz

B C D E F
B C D E F (pbk.)
Printed in Hong Kong

For Danielle

The AMAZON PAPERS

1

"WHILE YOU ARE draining your crankcase," Aunt Blanche observed, "other young women are draining the cup of life."

It wasn't even my crankcase. The car was my mother's. My mother, plainly, had been confiding in her sister Blanche, who was telling me, in her own way, that they were worried. They were worried because I was spending most of my summer under the Chevy or out on the playing fields instead of on the telephone or cruising the mall.

If my mother had had any suspicion that I even intended to drain the cup of life, romantically speaking, she would have probably railroaded me into a girls' school, or even a nunnery. But she knew Blanche could afford to talk the way she did with no danger of inciting me. Here I was, pushing sixteen, without so much as a school tardy or a missed curfew in my past.

I slid out from under the '88 Celebrity. "You're talking this way because my birthday's coming up in a few weeks, right?"

"You want people saying when you're a crotchety spinster of uncertain years, 'How beautiful that Iris Hoving gave up a life of her own to be a comfort to her mother in their old age'?"

I flushed. I flush as easily as a two-hundred-dollar commode. "Aunt Blanche, spinster is an archaic term."

"So I've got archaic sensibilities."

She had me there. While she's only eight years older than my mother, she clearly refuses to accept the times we live in.

My aunt still wears Chanel suits, with the straight skirts and little straight jackets, that she picks up from thrift stores and consignment shops. She stands about five feet six in the canvas faux espadrilles she buys at the Payless Shoe-Source. Her hair is thick and wild and showing no gray, and her face bears a disconcerting resemblance to that of Caesar Augustus. This is prepossessing in a woman of fifty, but it doesn't have the impact it would have if she were my height. On the other hand, in her day women probably would have chosen to have the face of an antique Roman emperor rather than be five feet ten.

Blanche had never married. When she was young, she was a reporter at a local newspaper. Then, when she was thirty, she got a job with the U.S. Information Service in Saudi Arabia. After a few years, when I was about nine, she came back here, to this flat Midwest town, and got an apartment a few blocks from my mother's house.

Blanche never talked about those years abroad. I used to imagine that she'd had a doomed love affair with an Arab sheikh who died in a Bedouin skirmish, or maybe with a war correspondent who had a tragic, fatal drinking problem. Now that I'm older, I realize it's more likely that there was a government cutback and she was simply surplus.

I was not about to let her get away with telling me I had no meaningful existence. "Aunt Blanche, I've got a life of my own. I have school. I have work."

"Washing floors and windows for neighbors who aren't fussy about streaks. I'm talking social life. When you're not disemboweling carburetors or breaking your bones on the ski slopes, you're reading philosophy. Iris, who ever heard of a fifiteen-year-old who reads *philosophy*?"

I stood. I looked down at my aunt. "There

was a time when everybody cared about philosophy. There was this disciple of Heracleitis, the Ionian philosopher—"

"Right away, you're talking B.C."

"Once, when Heracleitis said, 'You cannot step twice into the same river, for fresh waters are forever flowing in on you,' somebody came back with 'You can't step into the *same* river *once*.' This upset the disciple so much that he never spoke another word for the rest of his life."

"You want Latin philosophy," she warned, "I'll give you Latin philosophy."

"Heracleitis was Greek."

"Greek I don't speak. Carpe diem. You know what that means in Latin? 'Seize the day.'"

My face burned like the pages of a Harlequin romance. "You want me to be a topless dancer or something? Is that what you want?"

Blanche looked up at me. "The mind," she said, "boggles."

As she retreated to the kitchen, I yelled after her, "Would anybody call Sigourney Weaver *buxom*? Does Bridget Fonda fill a B cup, even?"

I finished the oil change, lingering until I was sure my aunt had left.

When I came into the house, my mother announced, "I ordered us a pizza."

In some families this might be a treat. In mine, it happens twice a week, anyway, so that I was not excited but relieved.

4

My mother does not waste time with trivial things like sifting or measuring. Biting into anything she bakes from scratch is a test of raw bravado. Those lumps of baking soda are still a shock, even more than the clots of cinnamon or nutmeg that have sat so long in their cans they've gone solid.

Without takeout, send-out, and a microwave, we'd have been a piteous pair. I know my mother has pressures with her work. There are always payrolls to make out. Since she's an accountant, her crazy times are in the weeks before April fifteenth. Once income taxes are filed and late returns are dealt with, she has a kind of hiatus. She weeds the yard and cleans the house, but her cooking is still erratic.

Sometimes I wonder what our life was like when my father was alive. Since I was only three when he died, I don't remember. She tells me about him—he was a salesman, loved us, worked hard, died at thirty-five when a dune buggy rolled on him. There are pictures of him in our family albums but not on the wall. I don't know whether the marriage was so wretched she wants to forget it, or whether she loved him so much she can't bear to think about him.

While I showered and changed, I thought about my conversation with my aunt and reflected that Sigourney Weaver even wore the same kind of underwear I did, at least in *Alien*.

My mother was still at her desk in the kitchen. "In my day," she said, "there were a lot of girls who didn't . . . develop . . . until sixteen or even seventeen." This was supposed to be comforting.

Actually, I seldom worried about not having much of a bosom. I'm lean all over, but my bones are respectably cushioned, and I'm not so flat as some of the girls I know. But when you've got your mother in an apologetic mode, you might as well make the most of it. I merely nodded, trying to look stoic and long-suffering.

"They've got Foster cooking, so you'll have to pick it up," she added.

Knowing how my mother thinks in arabesques, I understood that she was referring back to the pizza.

"I just fixed the car for you!"

"I still don't trust it," she said.

My mother feels intense about her Chevy. It's not a love-hate relationship, but a love-suspicion thing. From what I gather, my father left a lot of medical bills and no insurance. My mother, for as long as I can remember, has worked hard to support us. It was a big deal when she could buy the little house we live in now, and when we got a refrigerator that didn't leak, and, finally, when she got this car.

She's as compulsively conscientious a car owner as she is a parent. She's never missed one of my school events. Parent-teacher conferences are sacred to her. I get my teeth checked every six months and a physical every year.

The Chevy, too, got regular checkups, until I convinced my mother that I could take care of it capably—and cheaper. I washed it; I waxed it; I tended to the maintenance and fooled around with the engine and tried to convince her that every strange sound it made was not a death rattle.

WALKING TO Xiang Lo's, I fumed. When my mother said she didn't trust the car, after I'd spent hours slaving over it, she as much as implied she didn't trust me. I fix the car, I thought, and then I have to walk to the pizza parlor. When I'm sixteen and get my license, will she say she doesn't trust me to drive? What did everybody want from me? I'm a straight-A student, auto mechanic, hotshot athlete, but I'm getting this retrograde pressure to be . . . what?

I had a nagging fear that I *knew* what, that somewhere in the 1970 recesses of their psyches, my mother and aunt wanted me to be more like my cousin Ellie. Ellie was blond, with wide green eyes and ivory skin and her 106 pounds artistically distributed over a five-feet-two-inch frame. I couldn't help suspecting that if my mother had been able to custom-design a daughter, it would have been Ellie.

I walked a little faster.

It was getting on toward five o'clock, the kind of June afternoon when the heat keeps building up until six and then ebbs slowly with the light, so that at eight it's barely edging into dusk and you don't even need a sweater.

Kids were out in front yards playing in wading pools or sprinklers. This was not a neighborhood of central air-conditioning or swimming pools, except for those plastic above-ground deals a family around here would go in hock for years to buy. The houses were all like ours, built in the fifties, with single-car garages and single bathrooms tiled in maroon and pink. Most of the yards were tended decently, a few with pink plastic flamingos and plastic birdbaths.

After a couple of blocks, the houses gave way to a safe but rundown shopping area, with a mom-and-pop grocery, a shoe repair shop, a drugstore, and Xiang Lo's.

By the time I walked into the pizzeria, I was pretty well fumed out.

Over by the ovens, Foster Prizer was battering a big hunk of dough.

Foster Prizer was at least eighteen, as tall as I, lean and dangerous looking, with his black curly hair, blue eyes, and earring, and the cheekbones of a Tartar.

Normally, Foster delivered pizza, but today he was making it.

Before I could get my heart and voice under control, Xiang Lo came out from behind the ovens. Xiang Lo is around fifty, and when I was little, I wished he could be my grandfather, probably because he always gave me peppermint candies when my mother brought me in to pick up dinner.

"Iris!" Xiang Lo's voice was vibrant with urgency now. "Iris, I need you!"

I get this all the time from men. Show me a male who's having trouble with a carburetor, a term paper, or loading a refrigerator onto a flatbed, right away he thinks of me.

Xiang Lo went on to explain that his bowling team was up against the Pink Poodle Pet Groomers for the championship, and his cook and star bowler was out with the flu.

Bowling is not my idea of a fulfilling experience, but I'm a pushover for anybody who's desperate. That's why I let myself get drafted for neighborhood softball and touch football. Limping off dusty lots with applause and sinister tintinnabulation ringing in my ears, I often wonder if I'm a little too sympathetic to other people's problems.

"But I'm not a Xiang Lo employee," I pointed out.

"I'm deputizing you," he countered. "You know Foster here. Foster, you can pick her up tonight. She's on your way."

I felt as scared, and as excited, as if I were about to run a marathon again. *Foster Prizer would pick me up!*

Barely taking his slate blue eyes off the tomato sauce, Foster asked my address and said he'd swing by at seven.

As I walked home, I might have hugged the warmth of his pizza close to my bosom, except for the risk of sauce slippage and except for being seriously ticked off.

My address? He asked for my address? He must have delivered pizza to our house a dozen times in the last six months! Was I invisible? Could I not compete with mushrooms and artichoke hearts?

Maybe he's just playing it cool, I told myself. And I would have to play it very, very cool in telling my mother I was going out with a high school dropout who had a reputation.

On the other hand, I reasoned, how could she veto my helping Xiang Lo and his wife? They were so dedicated to bowling, they'd closed the pizzeria every Tuesday at six for as long as I could remember. And what other pizza parlor used soy cheese instead of the real stuff? Where else could a vegan like me eat pizza with a clear conscience? But for Xiang Lo's pizza, my mother's arteries would be a sludge of cholesterol and bovine growth hormones. Anyway, how could she object to one of their employees just picking me up and dropping me home?

A woman who *harasses* her fifteen-year-old daughter to be a social animal has no complaints coming if her child starts seeing an older man who is not heavily into education.

Walking into my kitchen, I decided that the way to approach the subject was straight on. "So I'm going out tonight," I announced as I handed my mother the box.

"Good." She got two mugs from a cupboard.

Good? Just *good*? She did not care enough to ask who, where, why? "With Foster Prizer from the pizzeria."

"I know." She handed me the mugs. "Xiang Lo called to tell me. He said he and Mrs. Xiang would bring you home. Nice boy, Foster. Always so polite."

She could at least be a little bit concerned. "Ma, he's a high school dropout. Everybody knows—"

"He's probably working to help out at home, Iris." She tossed me a roll of paper towels.

"Don't you even *worry* about me?"

"Sweetie, I trust you completely. It's not as if you're going out on a *date* with somebody that . . . that . . ."

"That what?" I pressed.

"That . . . you know. That . . . like James Dean," she said.

"James Dean has been dead for generations." I tore off four paper towels, two for place mats, two for napkins.

"There's that same renegade look to Foster. But his giving you a ride to the bowling alley is no cause for concern."

I tried not to seem preoccupied while we ate, but I had to contend with the onion issue. If I picked the onions off my pizza, my mother might suspect I expected Foster to get close enough to inhale my breath. On the other hand, if I ate the onions, and Foster ... No. No. Even onion breath would not be as embarrassing as explaining to my mother why I was picking the onions off my pizza. I'd just have to gargle vigorously with her blue mouthwash every few minutes until he arrived, and maybe pinch a few cloves from her spice cabinet and hope they weren't as moldy as the cabinet was dusty.

As soon as we'd tidied the kitchen, which meant rinsing the mugs and tossing the towels and pizza box into the recycling bin, I took a shower and gargled at length, and then went to my room to survey my closet.

How do you dress to fill in on a bowling team when the most devastating male you have ever known is fetching you ... and a middle-aged couple is bringing you home? I knew flash and glitz were out. Anyway, there was no flicker of flash, no glimmer of glitz, in my wardrobe.

I settled on a shirt that didn't make me look flat and jeans that did, except for the butt.

What will I say to him? I aimed a brush at my hair, which had been recently whacked at an EIGHT DOLLARS NO WAITING NO APPOINTMENT NO MAKING A SCENE ON THE PREMISES OVER THE RESULT place. What if he's surly and silent because the boss made him pick me up? What if he knows I'm only fifteen? What if he's embarrassed to be seen with me even at stoplights?

I heard the telephone ringing in the kitchen. See? I told myself. See? Already he's reconsidered.

My mother came in, trailing the phone cord, her hand over the mouthpiece. "Foster Prizer."

My mouth went dry. My palms were all slippery as I took the phone. "Um . . . yes?"

"Iris, I've got a problem. My Maria won't start. It may be her carburetor. Can you make it to the Bowlarama on your own?"

What could I say? I couldn't let Xiang Lo down. Besides, if I didn't go, Foster might think I was staying at home because he wasn't picking me up. I turned to my mother. "Could you drive me to the Bowlarama or should I take a bus?"

"You never know what kind of people you'll meet on a bus in the evening. If you're sure the Chevy's not going to blow up on us, I'll take you. Let me get something on."

"I'll be there," I told Foster, and hung up.

At least I wouldn't have to worry what to say to him in the car.

I WAS SILENT on the way to the Bowlarama. Had Foster stood me up or was his carburetor truly balky? If he had stood me up, was it my looks or my personality or merely that he was afraid of a half hour's commitment?

The Bowlarama wasn't in a really bad neighborhood, just a slightly unsuccessful one. We passed a Food 4 Less market, a third-run movie house that was closed for repairs, and a fabric store gone out of business. The streets, like the parking lot, were full of potholes, but you never saw gangs or graffiti around. Somehow, the area had stayed almost fifties wholesome.

The Bowlarama, a glorified Quonset hut, faced a parking lot the size of a city block packed with everything from family station wagons to decrepit heaps. I could see Xiang Lo's delivery van.

My mother pulled up to the entrance. I knew there was no sense asking her to let me out far enough away so nobody would notice that my *mother* had brought me. But the night was dark, the lot feebly lit, and my mother was, despite her casual ways, not entirely devoid of protective instincts.

When I got out of the car, I said, "I may be late, Ma."

"Make the most of it," she said, and drove

14

away. Not a caution, not a warning, not a curfew.

Too late to nudge her into parenting classes, I thought. But as I edged through the crowd, my mood softened. My mother had had her share of disappointments. Mainly me.

By the time I was eleven, I towered over my cousin Ellie, who was, at twenty-two, well into marriage and maternity. In the hope I might be some long-stemmed American Beauty in the bud, my mother enrolled me in ballet classes.

I was twelve, the bottoms of my long stems snug in size-eight Capezios, when my ballet instructor told me, "Iris, you've got style, you've got power, you've got drive. If you were a man, you might be another Nureyev, a Baryshnikov." He looked up at me, the death of a dream shadowing his face.

After ballet, my mother talked about getting me piano or violin lessons, but we couldn't afford to buy either instrument. That had been the advantage of ballet—we already had a floor.

So I spent more time on athletics, especially after my aunt bought me a pair of skis at a thrift store.

THIS NIGHT, at least, I didn't disappoint anybody.

The Xiang Lo team cheered my every strike, my every spare. When the scores were totaled, I was clapped on the shoulder, slapped on the back, hugged . . . If I'd been older, everybody

15

probably would have tried to buy me a beer. As it was, I had three colas and an orange soda shoved in front of me.

"You move with a lot of class, Iris." Foster Prizer slid into the booth beside me. "Has anybody ever told you you're a natural athlete?"

I nodded, hoping he might take my blush for the glow from healthy exercise. I forced myself to speak. "My coach, Bernie Bevins. He discovered me."

Foster rested a muscular arm on the back of the booth. "Wow! Like Springsteen and Patti Scialfa."

"No. Bernie was only interested in my body. All he saw in me was bone and muscle and a shot at the Olympics." I could feel the warmth from Foster's arm. "But I had an accident while I was training for the giant slalom." I was fourteen, and there was a blond on the ski patrol who did tai chi every morning. I was navigating the slalom when I saw him watching me, and my heart turned over in my chest. This was just before the rest of me turned over on my skis. By the time I'd gone through six months of surgery and casts and rehabilitation, I decided that I didn't have the clear, cold, single-minded dedication to be an Olympian. Besides, we didn't have health insurance, so my mother had to get a second mortgage on the house. It was the only serious accident I'd ever had, but I didn't have the heart to risk running up more medical bills. I stuck to cheaper athletics, where the worst case would be a simple fracture that could be set in the ER.

"Iris Hoving!" somebody called over the loudspeaker. "Telephone! Emergency!"

My cousin Ellie was on the line. "Iris, Mercy Hospital just called. It's your mother. They say she put her head in the oven . . ."

Leaving the receiver dangling and the team back in the booth, I ran out of the Bowlarama, out of the neon lights, and into the black night.

At least I hadn't lost my endurance. When I dashed into Mercy Hospital, I was sweating but barely panting. I was sent from desk to desk until Dr. Woodridge found me. He was a year older than when I'd seen him last, but you never forget the man who has reconstructed your tibia and fibula, your radius and ulna.

He looked the same, faintly weary but in control—in control of events and himself. He was tall, with black hair, deep-set gray eyes, and a nose that had been broken and set casually, slightly flattened across the bridge, so that he looked both elegant and macho.

"My mother . . . ," I gasped.

"She's fine, Iris." He explained what had happened.

"Wait a minute," I interrupted. "You're saying she put her head in the oven and threw her *back* out of whack?"

He nodded.

"And she's been sent home already?"

"All she needs now is rest."

I DIDN'T ENCOUNTER anybody menacing on the bus. I was in such turmoil, I wouldn't have noticed if I had. *What had driven my mother to put her head in the oven?* How could I have been so dense not to have picked up any hint of her despair? How could I have left her alone when she was at the end of her rope?

Our front door opened only inches before the chain stopped it. "Ma, wait! Don't do anything! We can talk!" I threw myself forward, shoulder first.

Stumbling past my cousin Ellie, who had snatched up her two little boys and flattened herself against the foyer wall, I staggered into my mother's room. "I'm here, Ma."

"Dear Lord," she groaned. "I know it."

She lay on the old double bed, her back propped against the half-round headboard, pillows under her knees.

"Why, Ma? Why? It wasn't anything I did, was it? No matter what you were going through, we could have worked it out. But to stick your head in the *oven* . . ."

"I put my head in to spear a pizza slice that fell through the rack."

I sat on the bed, stunned, barely noticing her wince. "You mean you didn't . . ."

She patted my cheek gently. "Iris, we have an electric stove. Call the Xiangs and explain. They phoned here wondering what happened to you. Why don't you go talk to your cousin before she goes."

"And leave you all alone?"

"For as long as possible."

STILL, THE SCARE made me realize that my mother and I had a communication problem. We never really shared secrets. We never had long conversations about the meaning of life.

For the next days, I gave up all my jobs and teams to look after Mom. I didn't go anywhere with my friends. I cut my phone conversations short. The Xiangs sent over pizza as a get-well gift, but I was too preoccupied to murmur more than a thank-you when Foster delivered it.

The rest of the time, I made home-cooked meals. I brought my mother juice and vitamin pills every few hours. I read philosophy to her. I turned off the television set, which I'd brought into her room, right after the ten o'clock news, so she could get a good night's sleep. I kept after her to do isometric exercises so she wouldn't suffer any muscle wasting while she was in bed.

A week after her accident, she canceled her appointment with Judson Woodridge, saying she was too tired to get up.

The same afternoon, I got a call from him. "I talked to your mother on the telephone, Iris. I'm coming over tonight."

When a hotshot bone surgeon volunteers to make a house call, you know something is going on. A man who drives a silver Maserati is no simple country doctor.

I knew that if I asked Ellie or Blanche to come over, my mother would suspect that Woodridge had something grim to tell her.

I kept an eye out for his car that evening. When I saw it pull up, I met him on the porch. "Give it to me straight, Doc."

"Your mother needs a vacation."

"Vacation?" The man had come to the house as a social director? "Vacation? In her condition? How could we afford it?" And then I thought, this is my *mother*. If I have to wash more floors and windows, if I have to drop out of high school and get a full-time job, it will only be a few years of sacrifice. Sure, I might end up a pinch-faced woman with premature frown lines and seething subterranean hostilities, but I could worry about all that in the long evenings to come. "Where would I take her?"

"Not a vacation with you," Judson Woodridge said. "A vacation *from* you."

Mother looked relieved when we walked into her room.

"I've talked to Iris," he said.

"You're a kind and devoted nurse, dear," Mother assured me, "but I'm afraid I'm wearing you out. You're so dedicated. So . . . zealous."

I could feel my face go pink as a lawn flamingo. "You're telling me I have the nursing skills of . . . of a water buffalo. That's what you're telling me."

"Oh, no, love." Her voice was warm, but devoid of any real conviction. "It's just that perhaps I'm at the point now where I need a bit of benign neglect, maybe a change of scene . . ."

"How can you go anywhere with a bad back?" I demanded. "You'll walk funny."

"I've talked to your cousin Ellie," she said. "If anybody needs to get away as much as I do, it's Ellie. Those kids drive her crazy."

"A vacation, with two little boys?" Looking from my mother to Woodridge, I understood. I saw the face of conspiracy. "You plotted this, didn't you? This whole trip. The two of you. Ma, I've never willingly spent an hour with little kids since *I* was one! I'm not even sixteen! They ought to be in day care, anyway."

"You remember, sweetie. Ellie took them out for the summer so she could spend more quality time with them."

"They were *expelled,* right after they stuffed toilet paper down the toilets and flooded the building. And if Ellie wanted all that quality time with them, why is she so eager to dump them on me?"

Mother was patient. "Because she's been spending—"

I held up my hand. "I know . . . all that quality time with them."

My mother's voice was soft and implacable. "It's all arranged. Blanche will come in nights. You only have to watch the boys days."

"Why can't she watch them days?" I strove to keep my pitch below a level audible only to dogs.

"You'd put a woman her age through that?" Mother asked.

"But you'd leave those kids in the care of a water buffalo?" I rasped.

"Children," she said reassuringly, "are resilient. And you have all that youth and strength."

"Aunt Blanche," I warned darkly, "will tell me every night that females over fourteen ought to be engaged. She'll tell me about all the dates you had at my age. She may let slip things you thought would never get out."

"Blanche is the salt of the earth," my mother said calmly.

"The garlic salt," I growled. My aunt was a strong-minded woman with powerful convictions about everything, including religion, politics, music, sickness, and health. She preached her own cures for every ailment: echinacea for flu, slippery elm for sore throat, and all with garlic—garlic for every ill.

My mother refused to take offense. Faced with the prospect of separation from her firstborn, her only-born, she murmured, still placid, "Blanche adores you. And I will feel perfectly at ease knowing she's looking after you and the boys."

"After sundown." I strode from the room. I'd devoted myself to my mother these past few days, and all she wanted was to get away with my cousin, who wouldn't know a hot pack from a six-pack. I'm not one for crying, but I felt as if I had a softball wedged in my larynx.

Woodridge followed me. I should have realized then, if not much, much earlier, that his interest was more than professional. His voice was low, his words tough. "Either your mother goes alone, which is absolutely against my advice, or she goes with your cousin. But I'm not going to have you nurse my patient right into a rest home." He gazed at me closely. "You look as if you could use some time off, yourself."

"With my cousin's spawn on my hands?" Why bother to hide my bitterness?

"You'll have your aunt here nights," he reminded me.

"Great. Great. That gives me only daylight hours in bondage."

He was not moved. "My daugher Fauncine is a perfectly capable baby-sitter. I'm sure she'd be happy to watch the boys for an hour or two some afternoon. You still have my home number?"

He beeped.

As he groped in his pocket for his pager, I said, "The phone is in the kitchen."

He spoke briefly, then left the house.

Watching him stride out to his Maserati, I was a Crock-Pot of emotions.

Here was my mother going off on vacation. And was she bringing me, her only child? No. She was taking my cousin Ellie, leaving me with Ellie's rug rats and a sitter! So which is it? I thought. I'm old enough to have carpet sharks dumped on me, but not old enough to be left alone all night. And did anybody ask whether I might have had plans of my own? No. My own mother thinks I'm a mere observer in the battle of the sexes.

Ha.

I realize that, almost sixteen, five feet ten, with all the feminine wiles of an Amazon, I could emerge untouched from spring break at Fort Lauderdale.

Not that guys ignore me. I can put my finger on an engine problem faster than I can diagram a sentence. When a male notices a suspicious noise under the hood, when he senses that his schuss seems sloppy, when he needs to tighten up a term paper, right away he turns to me.

Of course, there have been those who think of me as more than one of the boys. They tend to be under five feet five, long on enthusiasm, but short on subtlety—as if, because I'm tall and strong and capable, I'm to be approached like the north face of the Matterhorn. I think of it as the Mount Everest Syndrome, the male's urge to conquer something monumental.

My thoughts returned to Judson Woodridge. Though the idea was stunning, it was clear there was something behind this doctor's special interest in us, something more than Hippocrates mentions.

I wondered. I mused. I pondered.

I made my mother a cup of hot chocolate. She'd been trying for months to lose weight, but a middle-aged woman has no business trying to pare herself down to supermodel svelte. I walked into her room, the chocolate barely slopping onto the saucer. "I know you're pretending to be asleep."

I raised the pillows so she had to sit up. I pressed the cup and saucer into her hands. "If you don't mind a question from a water buffalo, what do you suppose is going on with old Woodridge?"

"Going on?"

I tried to keep my voice cool and clinical and faintly bemused. "I think he may have a . . . personal interest in our family."

Mother blotted the saucer with a Kleenex. "Good. Maybe he'll shave his bill."

I don't know. Maybe parenting classes would be too narrow. Maybe sensitivity training was the ticket.

MY COUSIN ELLIE snapped up my mother's invitation like a chameleon greeting a fly. Two years ago, Ellie's husband, a bank teller, left for work promising to do something about the car payments. What he did was fly to Belize alone at the end of the day with half a million of the bank's dollars.

Everybody told Ellie how bravely she held up.

Presently, she's juggling the affections of her city councilman, the investigator assigned to her husband's case, and a soccer player from Paraguay who wants her to marry him and put him through veterinary school. I would say she was holding up just fine.

Five days later, we took a taxi to the airport,

where her little Alvin and Pete played tag around and over passengers and luggage and tried to eat cigarette butts out of the sand in the floor-stand ashtrays—and made me think that there's a lot to be said for a woman remaining unfulfilled, womb-wise.

Standing there waiting for the boarding call, I wondered if I should ask Ellie to cue me in on her rug rats' ages, but I didn't have the nerve. I'd known them all their lives, after all. Pete had to be around five or six. He was slender like his mother, with curly blond hair and, when he was not running amok in public, a kind of solemn look. Alvin couldn't be more than two, I figured. He had a round face, straight black hair cut Prince Valiant style, and brown eyes with a stare so unwavering it could unhinge a panther.

I glanced again at the pages of instructions she'd given me. "There's got to be more to it."

"They'll love you," she assured me. "Kids are intuitive."

Intuitive? They were eerie. A second before boarding was announced, they threw themselves at their mother, winding arms and legs around her like crazed kudzu vines.

My mother kissed me, and Ellie tried to get disentangled enough to hug me, and then we had to pry her free of her boys.

It took me half an hour to get my new wards to the bus, with Alvin hanging over my right arm and Pete dragging from my left hand, both boys limp and blubbering.

In the hope they might stupefy themselves with empty calories, I took them to a fast-food place and told them to order anything they liked for lunch.

Later, as I slipped from behind the table to shake relish off my leg and collect the french fries scattered across the floor and blot ketchup puddles off the vinyl seat, I reflected that my mother and Ellie were probably being served a microwaved gourmet banquet by some tall, intense flight attendant who would sooner or later suggest that Ellie send him through air traffic controller school.

"WHY IS IT?" I asked, examining Alvin's fang marks on Pete's wrist when we got home. "Why is it that small children turn savage on public transportation? Is this a characteristic of your species?"

Ignoring me, Pete marched into my mother's room and, as if equipped with some electronic homing device, immediately laid his hand on the television remote and called up a program replete with sex and violence.

I stepped in front of the set. "We are going for wholesome entertainment, kid."

He tried to edge around me. I turned the television off.

He scrunched his eyes almost shut, his face going purple.

I called up every feral instinct in my limbic system. "Listen, I think my mother left some disquieting desserts in the freezer—confections that no human under thirty should be allowed to ingest."

They followed me to the kitchen. They gnawed on unthawed chocolate éclairs while I telephoned Aunt Blanche. "I was just wondering if maybe you could come over a little early."

"Oh, sweetie," she wheezed. "I'm flat on my back with a flu that hit me like a freight train. I'm trying to think who else I could get for you until my garlic kicks in. There's Mrs. Rutching down the block . . ."

"No, that's all right," I said hastily. Mrs. Rutching whiled away her spare time turning her garden hose on cats that crossed her lawn. "I'll ask one of my friends."

"Absolutely not!" she rasped. "That would make it a pajama party! No friends. Your mother would want some mature, responsible person. I'll call Mrs. Rutching."

"Wait. Wait. I know of . . . of a very responsible person. Not a friend."

"Is your mother acquainted with her?"

"It's . . ." I thought fast. "It's a relative of Dr. Woodridge's."

"Oh, good. Now, if for any reason she can't

come, you call me, and I'll get someone from my investment club to stay with you. Otherwise, don't phone unless you need to, honey. The more I rest now, the sooner I'll be up and around."

I had not actually lied, I told myself. I did know of a responsible person. There was no need mentioning that I had no idea how old Woodridge's daughter was and no intention of calling her.

I yanked Alvin's arm out of the microwave.

"I was only going to X-ray him," Pete protested.

I lifted Alvin off the counter. "I can see that nobody has ever taught you guys the first thing about martial arts."

By dinnertime I had them so worn out, they barely snarled at being forced to wash their hands.

In a few short hours, in less than a day, I had learned to manipulate innocent children through bribery and trickery.

Not bad, I thought.

I decided, while I was sponging Tiger's Milk and sprouts off them, I might as well get them into their pajamas.

"Aren't you going to change him?" Pete asked as I tried to figure out which were the arms and which the legs of Alvin's sleepers.

"Into what?"

Pete rolled his eyes toward the ceiling. "Change his *diapers*."

I looked around me for Ellie's instruction sheets. "He wears diapers under pajamas?"

"Under everything."

"The kid must be two years old," I protested.

"Twenty-two months." Digging through the supplies Ellie had left, Pete handed me a wasp-waisted panel that looked to be several layers of paper and plastic. "You put a fresh one on him at night and whenever he needs it."

"How can you tell when he needs it?"

"Feel him."

"Like . . . come here, Alvin. *Yeccch*."

I had just wrestled the kid into his diaper and nightclothes when the telephone rang.

It was Foster Prizer, his voice vibrant with need. "Iris, all you have to say is yes."

I heard him out. "Foster," I said, "I need a little time. How about eight?"

After I hung up, I managed to assess the situation.

I was certainly not going to call my poor ailing aunt just to upset her. I had a feeling that, despite all that "cup of life" talk, she might not be as serene as my mother was about Foster.

There was no point laying a dilemma on Blanche when she needed to summon all her inner resources to heal herself.

33

While she had never forbidden me to go out with Foster, she had said that I couldn't have any of my friends over. If I did enlist one to sit with Alvin and Pete, and my aunt found out, she might fairly accuse me of deliberately defying her.

Besides, a friend would want to know whom I was going out with. Then I'd have to listen to "He's so gorgeous!" "Do you think he really *likes* you?" "What will your mother say?"

Judson Woodridge had given us his unlisted number when I was released from the hospital.

"Is Fauncine there?" I asked the female who answered his phone.

"Speaking." She sounded as if she suspected telemarketing fraud.

"My mother is a patient of your father's," I introduced myself, "and I'm desperate."

"Dad," she called, "it's a desperate patient!"

Woodridge was on the line at once.

"It's Iris Hoving," I told him quickly, "and I'm only desperate because I have to go out tonight."

Even over the telephone, you can recognize an icy silence.

"My bowling team needs me," I explained. "Tonight is the play-off for the regional championship, and they're still short-handed."

"Bowling." He sounded as if I'd confessed to a taste for accordion concerts. "Isn't your aunt there?"

"Well, she . . ." If I tell him, I thought, I might have him calling the nurses' registry to find me a night keeper. "She . . . she's resting. And the boys are pretty active. I know it's short notice . . ."

"That's all right," Fauncine, on the extension, broke in.

My mother had left Blanche a check, left the kitchen stocked with groceries, and given me two hundred dollars for emergencies. I had a feeling she wouldn't consider bowling an emergency. But, then, she didn't see Foster through my eyes.

Again I dragged out every garment I owned. I reminded myself that this was not an actual date, that Foster was calling at Xiang Lo's behest, and that the idea was to dress *appropriately*.

My mother had taken all her makeup with her. What am I doing, I asked myself fiercely, without so much as a blusher to my name? Fifteen years I have spent being responsible, being a student, being an athlete, without even preparing for the possibility that someday I might want somebody to see me as A Woman.

I had a mother who had abandoned me to go on a Caribbean cruise with my cousin, a mother who had never bothered to teach me the facts of cosmetics. Tonight, I was all on my own.

I decided I'd better not experiment with makeup until I had more time.

35

Woodridge arrived at seven-thirty with Faun-cine, who looked to be all of fourteen. She was about five-feet-three and thin, almost wispy. Her hair was pale blond, her face a delicate oval, with hazel eyes. All in all, she reminded me of one of those repressed secondary characters in period novels—the heroine's friend or cousin, who either dies of consumption early on or languishes as a shadowy figure in her parents' household after being ruined by a dashing cavalry officer who jilts her for someone richer or prettier.

What had I done? How could I consign two high-spirited little boys to the care of a teenager who could throw Richard Simmons into a serious funk?

Woodridge volunteered to pick up his daughter at midnight, cautioned her not to let the boys disturb my aunt, and left before I could think of a tactful way to cancel the whole deal.

I introduced Fauncine to Pete and Alvin.

She acknowledged them with all the enthusiasm of a newcomer to a Gulag.

The boys trailed us like mongooses sizing up a cobra while I showed her around.

"Where's your aunt?" Her voice was as robust as her persona.

"What?"

"The aunt that's staying with you nights," she said.

"Oh, she . . . uh . . . she had to pop back to her house. I'll call her after you go." No need to say how many hours after.

Already, though, I was feeling tacky and sneaky for abusing the truth. If this is what being dazzled by a man does, I thought, it's no wonder women get bitter.

FOSTER ARRIVED at eight in a hearse.

I used to see him around town on a Harley-Davidson. But these days, of course, a Harley was a cliché among badass studs. Foster was cooler than mere cool. Foster was as cool as blue-cold crackling ice.

I could imagine, after he acquired his hearse, what a rush there must have been among his peers, all of them trying to buy defunct rolling stock from the mortuaries.

He even had what looked to be the original purple side drapes. Foster, with his unerring sense of style, had added nothing to the stark, sleek, shiny black body. Now, that's *mystique*.

I could tell he'd made a few modifications to the engine, though. Your average hearse doesn't sound like a Daytona challenger. I was surprised he'd had trouble with it, but I told myself that was not my problem.

As he strode to my door, I stepped back

quickly from the window so he wouldn't think I'd been watching for him, and I waited for his second knock before I opened the door.

He was wearing tight jeans, rocker boots, and a knit shirt, and his hair was still damp—I had to remind myself again that he'd been *assigned* to come for me.

I had to tell Fauncine twice where I'd be and when I planned to return.

Foster opened the passenger door—the live-passenger door—for me. My mother, I told myself, would certainly have approved of his manners.

As he slid into the driver's seat, I felt a fizzy excitement, more than just being out with a guy who was old enough to drive.

"I'm glad you could make it," he said. "So your mother's up and around?"

"My mother is having a ball."

The engine coughed for an instant, then rose to a guttural roar.

Even with that aggressive *rrrrmmmmmmrrr-mmmmmrrrmmmmm,* I was a little concerned about his spark plugs, but I thought that if I said anything, it might seem as if I were criticizing his hearse. I was silent.

So was Foster. I could tell that brief cough had him worried.

On the way to the Bowlarama, he filled me in

on the state of the tournament, the opposition, the lineup.

The Xiangs and the rest of their team greeted me as if I'd come to save the civilized world.

I tried to keep my mind on my game that night, but Foster practically hovered over me. Despite my mind's wandering, each ball I rolled kept its path. Even when I could barely concentrate, my body had its own discipline.

Later, when our team piled into a booth, Foster sat beside me. "You are fantastic, Iris."

I could feel my throat getting all fuzzy.

He leaned closer, his eyes dark, almost midnight blue, intense. "A born athlete. You ought to stick to your coach."

"I just don't want to give all my life to sports. There are so many other things. I want to get into a good college . . ."

He nodded, his gaze locked with mine. "Where have you applied?"

He had no idea I wasn't even sixteen!

"Have you picked a major yet?" he went on.

Foster Prizer is interested in my mind! I thought. He sees me as more than just the team's best chance at a trophy.

"I think I'd like to be a teacher," I confided.

He looked at me with respect.

Here is somebody, I realized, who looks beyond appearances, who sees me as something other than some kind of Amazon. Maybe we could talk about philosophy, even poetry.

"You going to teach PE?" he asked.

THE XIANGS drove me home. Foster offered, but they said my mother would probably feel better if they delivered me. I didn't mention that my mother was away. If they got a look at Fauncine and got to chatting at some time with my mother or my aunt, there was no telling what might come out.

As I trudged into the house, Woodridge's daughter trailed out from the kitchen. "It's not midnight yet."

"For me it is midnight, Fauncine. For me it will always be midnight."

"Did you have to pick up a body or something?"

I shook my head wearily. "It's his personal vehicle. An image thing. You can call your father to come get you."

"He's at a party. He'll pick me up at twelve and then dump me at home and go back out with whoever he's with." Her tone was matter-of-fact. "You want a cup of tea?"

I'd always thought of tea as something drunk by actors in old British movies, but I didn't have the heart to refuse.

The boys were sleeping like Botticelli cherubs in my mother's bed.

By the time I'd washed my face and changed into pajamas, Fauncine had tea all set out in the parlor.

"Lemon? Sugar?" She poured very seriously, almost ceremoniously. I had no idea where she'd picked up this formality—maybe from a book or a movie or some private school.

I was concerned about her drinking caffeine this late in the evening, but I didn't want to embarrass her by saying anything.

"I saw you win the diving competition in May," she confided solemnly. "I was supposed to present you with flowers, but they gave me hay fever."

"You dive?"

She shook her head. "Chlorine irritates my sinuses. Also, competition makes me nauseous. And I have trouble with my coordination."

By the time her father came, Fauncine had confided to me her thoughts about junior high, self-esteem, and her place in the universe.

This happens—younger kids looking up to you because you're a good athlete. I don't know if it ever happens because you're a great student. At any rate, it lays something like an obligation on you. When somebody admires you and trusts you with her deeper thoughts, you can't help feeling protective.

If I ever see her again, I thought, maybe we can do something about her posture.

4

I WOKE with Foster Prizer on my mind and small hungry boys in my face.

The kitchen was immaculate. "Hey—Fauncine washed the dishes from yesterday," I marveled.

"She knows all the words to 'I see by your outfit that you are a cowboy.'" Pete spoke as if she were his own invention. "And she puts Alvin's diapers on so they don't leak."

"Nevertheless, I'm beginning to think well of her."

Aunt Blanche called, sounding hoarse and tired. "Did you get someone to stay nights?"

"Yes," I said. Fauncine was someone. Until midnight was nights.

"Someone responsible?" she pressed.

"Absolutely." This I could say with complete honesty. "Listen, Aunt Blanche, can I do anything for you?"

"Oh, no, dear. I couldn't forgive myself if you caught this. And it would be terrible if I passed it on to Pete and Alvin."

I could agree with that. Having two healthy little boys on my hands was harrowing enough. "Could I bring you anything?"

"I have my television. And I'm eating my garlic."

By midmorning, I was out of paper diapers and pillowcases and dish towels, my thumb pitted with pinholes.

"THE KID IS a human monsoon." I pitched cartons of diapers into the supermarket cart.

"Could you buy some regular food?" Pete suggested.

"Listen, you've got veggie burgers, you've got Rice Dream, you've got spirulina. If you want to be an athlete, you've got to eat like one."

"I don't want to be an athlete," he said. "I want to be a stockbroker."

I hauled the boys over to the health food store and bought some fruit then telephoned Aunt Blanche. "I'll be by with a few things. I'll leave them on your porch."

Fortunately, she didn't come to the door. I felt guilty that I hadn't made her anything, but, on the other hand, my own mother had fled the country to escape my cooking—and, of course, to behave irresponsibly in a strange land or two.

Later, mopping Tofutti off the table, sweeping nutritional yeast off the floor, I reflected that there were hours to survive before bedtime. "How about going to the park?" I suggested. "Maybe you can pick up a *Wall Street Journal* lying around."

There were sailboats on the lake, waders in the shallows, and everywhere, everywhere, couples strolling, touching, whispering.

"I don't know," I mused. "Should you write off a perfectly gorgeous guy for just one failing?"

"You mean me?" Pete asked.

"What has your brother got in his mouth?"

"Teeth."

WHEN WE GOT HOME, the telephone was ringing.

It was Foster Prizer. "How do you feel about pool?" he asked.

"Xiang Lo has a pool team?"

"No, I thought you and I could play a few games. You can tell your mom it's a decent place. They don't serve liquor."

Wasn't it my own aunt who'd been after me to grasp life by the throat? As soon as I got the quiver out of my voice, I telephoned Fauncine. "Is there any chance you could sit tonight?"

It was easy.

44

Too easy.

She didn't even ask why my aunt kept absenting herself.

I bought frozen entrees at the market so I wouldn't feel I was exploiting Fauncine, and I picked up a few magazines with cover blurbs such as "Quick New Ways to Beauty." I decided to leave "Unlock the Sensuous Inner You" until I'd mastered "Fabulous Makeovers."

Again, fate seemed to be with me. There was a *Hercules* marathon on television. While Alvin napped and Pete watched *Son of Hercules against the Moon Men,* I studied the magazines.

As soon as Alvin woke, we went to the drugstore, where I spent forty-six dollars of my emergency money on makeup. An infinitesimal fraction, I told myself, of what a cruise for two was costing.

Judson Woodridge dropped off Fauncine that evening and left without coming to the door.

"Oh, wow," she greeted me. "I didn't know you were in a play!"

"I am made over, Francine."

She picked up Alvin. "What for?"

"To enhance my social life."

Her eyes remained fixed on my face.

"So?" I demanded.

"Well, you . . . You look kind of like a raccoon with a high fever."

I went back to the bathroom.

That's what we all need, I thought as I scrubbed my face, somebody honest and straightforward enough to tell us the unvarnished truth.

No wonder the kid is always free to baby-sit.

On the other hand, it was the customary me Foster had asked out. The new me might have confused him before he ever got to know the real me.

I smoothed on a little foundation, glossed up the old lips, and brushed on a couple of coats of mascara and a slash of blush. There was no law against looking *radiant*. I spritzed myself with my mother's Tumultuous cologne. Maybe I wasn't my usual self, but I would have recognized me, on close inspection. Even my mother would have, had she ever summoned the interest to scrutinize me.

The boys were watching *Hercules Versus the Mushroom People*. I knew it was irresponsible and selfish to plant small children in front of mindless television entertainment. I vowed I would make it up to them. Anyway, Fauncine would entertain them after I left.

The doorbell rang and I hurried into the parlor.

Fauncine would not have noticed if I'd strolled in sporting nothing but body paint, with my hair on fire.

Foster was wearing black jeans, a white shirt,

and a Bruce Springsteen bola tie. This guy could handle retro.

Fauncine stood annealed to the door frame, watching us walk to his hearse. If her father hadn't had a talk with her about life and men, I thought, somebody should. Soon.

The hearse's engine coughed. It groaned. It went silent.

Foster smote the dashboard so hard I wondered if we'd have to get his hand splinted. "I've been meaning to get this heap fixed."

"I could take a look at . . ." No! I told myself. We are projecting mystery and muted allure tonight.

As he struggled to start the engine, he got more tense. Finally, as if the words came with infinite pain, he asked, "I don't suppose you have Triple A?"

If we did, my mother either had the card, or left it with Blanche, I imagined.

I shook my head.

Even if I could find it, I doubted that Triple A would let a fifteen-year-old sign for starting somebody else's hearse.

I don't know. Maybe it was the feeling that a balky engine was murdering the whole mood of the evening. Maybe Foster Prizer had a way of driving a woman's brains right out her ears. To suggest we hop a bus would be like putting him down. Before I knew what I was saying, I heard myself murmur, "We could take my car."

I cannot explain it. I cannot defend it.

What do you expect from a person whose mother has run off to the Caribbean without giving her any cogent advice on men and how to deal with them?

Foster seemed embarrassed but relieved. He must have dreaded diving under the hood in his white shirt—and then maybe not being able to start the engine. But he didn't lose his cool. "We could do that," he said.

Talk about relieved. I was nervous enough having a hearse outside my house. I mean, it's generally considered an ominous vehicle. People notice. Moreover, Foster, even in the waning light, was enough to give every female on the block hormonal overload. If he stayed in sight too long, we might have had even Mrs. Rutching finding an excuse to come over.

And what about my poor aunt, home battling a virus? Sooner or later, Mrs. Rutching or one of her ilk would be sure to telephone and ask why there was a mortuary's vehicle parked outside my house.

"It would be a good idea," I said, striving to approximate his cool, "to put Maria in our garage. I wouldn't want any kids fooling around with her."

When I hurried into the house, Fauncine was

still standing by the front door. I snatched the car keys off the peg by the kitchen door. "We're going to need you, Fauncine."

I backed our car out of the garage, then explained to Fauncine how to steer a hearse. While she was too overwhelmed to look at Foster directly, I knew I'd better repeat my instructions slowly, carefully, and loudly.

With Foster and me pushing, we got Maria into the garage, and I could only hope no neighbors were watching and wondering whether I was going into the freelance funeral business.

THE POOL HOUR RESOURCES was way out on the far side of town, the raunchy side. I suffered all the way there, picturing some uninsured motorist piling into us. I told myself this was paranoia, not guilt. I had my learner's permit, I was with a licensed driver . . . Surely Xiang Lo wouldn't let anybody without a valid license deliver his pizzas. My mother had had no objection to Foster picking me up to go bowling. Why should she object to him taking me to a pool hall? A game of skill is a game of skill. As to my driving our car, wouldn't any mother prefer to have her daughter in the driver's seat?

Nonetheless, I could feel the muscles at the back of my neck tight as a trampoline.

The parking lot was packed with vehicles, from off-road behemoths to Camaros to Harleys.

Luckily, I was able to ease the Chevy between two compact cars.

It was my first pool hall, no bigger or noisier than the Bowlarama. On our right was a long, crowded bar; on our left, for as far as I could see, racks of cues. Down the center of the room were banks of pool tables.

Despite the banner FAMILIES WELCOME over the entrance outside, there were no children to be seen, or any adults one could conceive of as a parent. The clientele was heavy on teenagers, skinheads, and bikers, and almost exclusively male.

We were able to ease up to the bar without making physical contact with any of the customers.

Foster ordered two colas and turned sideways to the bar, facing me. "I'm glad you could come, Iris." His smile gleamed like fresh powder snow. "You seemed to get . . . preoccupied last night."

A slender brunette with a tiny waist, a Band-Aid of a skirt, shoes with ridiculous spike heels, and almost as much hair as Cher sidled between Foster and me. She didn't look to be more than eighteen, but while her bosom wasn't assertive enough to be vulgar, it was more than I could hope to attain in a decade.

"Hi, gorgeous," she accosted him.

"Oh, Zelma," he said.

"That's right. Zelma. As in, 'I'll call you,

Zelma.' Remember? That was three weeks ago."

Gazing over the newcomer's tumultuous hair at Foster, I felt like somebody peering from a camouflage blind.

"Zelma," Foster murmured, "I don't think you've met . . ."

She did not turn to acknowledge me. "Three weeks, Foster. 'I'll call,' you said, and I believed you. I mean, is that a laugh? I believed you."

I was feeling more and more uncomfortable. As the bartender put down our drinks, I picked them up. It is time, I told myself firmly, to stop this scene tactfully before it gets any more tawdry.

Zelma stepped even closer to Foster. "So here I am and here you are—let's settle this."

"Excuse me." I tried to ease around her. "Foster, why don't we find a place to sit down."

Zelma seized Foster by his Bruce Springsteen tie. Her elbow hit my right hand, and the cola sloshed down her shirt and my skirt.

I set the glasses on the bar. "Look, Zelma," I said quietly and reasonably. "You are crowding me, and you are embarrassing the person I'm with, and you need blotting."

"Hey, fella." A hulking skinhead with eyes the size and shade and expression of very pale agate marbles stepped up behind Foster and dropped a great slab of a hand on his shoulder. "You harassing these ladies?"

"Butt out, Bluto!" Zelma stamped her foot, just as Shirley Temple used to do. Only Shirley Temple was five years old. Shirley did not wear spike heels. Shirley stamped in an adorable little-girl pique, without putting a hundred and some pounds of weight into it.

And Shirley watched where she stamped.

It felt as if Zelma's spike heel went right through my instep.

"Oh, wow." Letting go of Foster's bola, she turned. "Was that your foot?"

As I leaned against the counter, my eyes closed against the agony and a primal rage, I heard old Bluto say, "Sorry, sir, but I'll have to ask you to leave."

And Foster snarled, in those immortal fighting words, "You and who else?"

Immortal, but not bright. As I opened my eyes, I saw two clones of that skinhead leviathan advance on Foster.

"Hey!" Zelma protested. "I'm not finished with him!"

But Foster was shoved and marched toward the door.

"They'll kill him!" I knew I should do something, but the pain in my instep knifed up my leg and my knee seemed to have come uncoupled.

"Nah," Zelma assured me. "Bouncers never kill anybody."

I felt my fingertips denting the Formica.

Zelma looked closely at me. "Are you going to faint or something? You're all pale and sweaty."

"Foster . . . ," I muttered.

"Kids get kicked out of here all the time without being hurt. We'd better leave, anyway. The longer you hang there on the counter, the more attention you're attracting." Cautiously, she edged closer. "Put your weight on me."

I did not have many choices. Though I would have preferred to socialize with a Tasmanian devil, I got an arm around her shoulder.

She sagged. "Not all your weight!"

Outside, I leaned against the wall, hot surges of pain washing over me. There was no sign of Foster, no sound of conflict. The night was starless and cool, the parking lot desolate, with the vehicles looming like shadowy hulks of defunct paleolithic beasts.

"I'll get my car," Zelma said. "Meanwhile, you'd better get out of your shoe before you have to cut it off. It felt as if your instep kind of crunched."

I sat on the pavement, my back against the front wall.

She was right about my foot. Already, it was swelling so much that I had trouble getting my sneaker untied.

Zelma pulled up in an ancient yellow Datsun.

She got out and looked down at my blue foot. "What a mess."

Holding me under the elbow, she helped me onto the split and ruptured passenger seat of the Datsun.

We drove in between all the rows of parked vehicles without finding Foster. We drove down all the streets in the area.

Meanwhile, the pain got worse, and the hour got late, and I had a baby-sitter whom I was paying by the hour.

"No telling where he is by now." Zelma turned on the inside car light and squinted at my foot. "I'd better run you to the hospital. You have health insurance?"

"Maybe they did get rough with Foster," I muttered through clenched teeth. "We'd better call the police."

"Hey, this is not a neighborhood where you step out of your car at night to make a phone call."

"Then get me back to my car."

"Are you kidding? You can't drive." She shook her head. "I'm really sorry, OK? I'm not admitting responsibility, but I'm trying to mitigate the damage. That's what the law says. It counts if you try to mitigate damages. If I let you drive, it would be a failure to mitigate."

"All right. All right." It would do no good to

yell at her, I knew. "You can drive me home in my car. I can't leave it."

"So who'll drive me back? Your parents are probably going to try to blame all this on me."

Even though this Zelma struck me as somebody who could have walked alone through the south Bronx at two A.M., I knew that in a neighborhood where it's not safe to go to a phone booth, you don't advise any female to step off a bus.

"Nobody's home. Nobody will be home." I tried to get my mind off my foot and focus it on the issues. "You'll get me and my car to my house, we'll call to be sure Foster's safe, even if we have to ask the police to look for him, and you can take a taxi back for your car."

She stopped the Datsun, leaving the motor on, and regarded me coolly. "You have cab fare on you?"

"No, but I . . ."

"Neither do I."

I tried to keep in mind that I was not injured as badly as I had been on the ski slopes. But, on the ski slopes, I was not trapped with the most extraordinarily irritating human being in the world. "I will give you the lousy cab fare as soon as I get home."

"How do I know you have it?"

Even as she spoke, I was trying to add up what

I'd spent so far. There was the restaurant I took the boys to, diapers, groceries, makeup, what I'd already paid Fauncine . . . "How much do you think it'll be?"

"Where do you live?"

"Thirty-eighth and Palm."

"A fortune, kid. That's a twenty-minute ride."

My face felt cold and damp. Under the sodium-vapor streetlight, encased in this decrepit Datsun, I could hear only sinister, muffled sounds from the dark streets around us.

There had to be some way to get both myself and the Chevy home. I could have Zelma take me back to the Pool Hour Resources. But what if the bouncers wouldn't let me back in? I could beg them to telephone one of my friends to come get me. No. No. I'd need two. I couldn't think of two friends who had more than learner's permits. That meant we'd have to get a parent to come along. Two parents. One to take me home, the other to drive the Chevy to our house. That way I would have somebody's mother *and* father asking what happened to my foot and what I was doing with my mother's car before I had my license, hanging out at a pool hall on these seamy streets. They'd probably insist on taking me to the hospital. They might feel obliged to call Aunt Blanche.

"Just drive me home in my own car. I'll figure some way to get your taxi fare."

"I don't think so," she said.

"Zelma, can't you *trust* anybody?" My indignation was not as vehement as it might have been, since I was already thinking that she might have to spend the night at my house and take a bus back for her Datsun in the morning. While I'd sooner entertain a werewolf than have this female under my family's roof, the thought of my aunt coming over in the morning and finding the Chevy gone gave me a powerful incentive to be less than candid with Zelma.

"Nah. Nobody's home at your house. I don't even know that you had permission to take the car. If you didn't, and I'm driving it, and we get in an accident . . ."

It was hopeless, I saw. Reasoning with this creature was like trying to paper-train a rhino.

"I'm running you to the hospital," she said.

"Not the hospital! Not the hospital! Home!" I cried, over the groaning of the Datsun's gears.

"I want to establish right now, for the record, that I am urging you to seek immediate medical atention. I'm warning you: I'm practically an attorney."

"I hear you, Zelma. Zelma, my family has lived in this town for generations. Everybody in this town knows my mother. They know us at the hospital. I do not want to explain, even to a health care professional, how this happened. Home."

"You have to sign a release, OK?"

"Just get me to my house." I figured, once I got there, I could concentrate on finding poor Foster. And if I found poor Foster, maybe I could get him to fetch the Chevy.

And so, without the high school dropout for whom I'd got my instep smashed in a squalid confrontation, I rode home with this pit bull of a female, abandoning my mother's car in a pool hall parking lot.

5

"OH, WOW! What happened?" Fauncine greeted us.

"It is not fit for young ears," I muttered as Zelma helped me to the sofa.

Fauncine didn't take her eyes off my left foot. "Foster Prizer called. He sounded worried."

"Did he leave a number?"

She handed me a slip of paper. "Your foot is all puffy and blue! What *happened*?"

"It's too sordid to discuss," I told her firmly.

She hurried into the kitchen and brought me the telephone. "Come on. What?"

"She was stomped in a pool hall after she flung her drink on a woman trying to relate to her date, all right?" Zelma flared.

"A *rumble?*" Fauncine punched in the numbers and handed me the telephone.

"A misunderstanding." I glared at Zelma as fiercely as a person in agony can.

"Ice." Fauncine rushed back to the kitchen.

"Hello?" Foster did, indeed, sound worried.

"Are you OK?" I asked.

"Iris! What happened? I went around to the back of the pool hall, but they wouldn't let me in. Then I waited by your car, but you never came."

"I had to take"—I leveled a killing glance at Zelma— "alternate transportation. Are you all right?"

"I think I cracked a couple of ribs, but otherwise no problem."

"I knew it. I knew it. You can sue that place."

"Well, they got cracked when I was trying to get in the back door. So, listen, should I take a bus over?"

"Foster, it's late, and Zelma's here. Maybe she could run you to the hospital."

There was a pause, then: "I would sooner risk a punctured lung."

I fended Zelma off as she reached for the phone. "Foster, I'm glad you're extant, but you'd better get your ribs checked."

"We'll talk later," he said, and hung up.

"He needs to see a doctor," I told Zelma.

"He'd never get into a closed space with me."

It would be cold and heartless to ask a person with fractured ribs to go fetch my car. Besides, he'd have to come by my house first for the keys.

Fauncine came in with ice cubes wrapped in dish towels and shoved a hassock toward me. "Put your foot up."

"Got any aspirin?" Zelma asked her.

I lifted my left leg with both hands and put my foot on the hassock. "I don't usually take any kind of . . ."

"For me." Zelma pressed delicate fingers to her temples. "I am talking major stress here."

Fauncine placed the ice carefully on my foot and then carried the telephone back to the kitchen.

Zelma nodded after her. "That kid is right out of *Invasion of the Body Snatchers*. You related?"

"So where do you plan to get your law degree, Zelma?" I inquired through my teeth. "San Quentin?"

"Listen, I was planning to start college next year." She sat down, which, in that skirt, was some feat. "I was delivering pizza and even saving some money. But I missed it by a nose. Literally."

"Not Xiang Lo's pizza?"

She shook her head. "Casa Nostra."

"Are you eighteen?"

"Seventeen. I borrowed my sister's ID," she said. "Anyway, one rainy night, Foster Prizer took a phone order for a dozen pizzas, and when I got to the address it was a vacant lot. I brought the whole dozen back, and after work the manager gave me six to take home. I figured I'd invite some friends over . . ."

"That would kill a slice of pizza right there," I observed.

"So I get off the bus at my corner juggling those soggy cartons in the rain, and I walk into a truck. Broke my nose. Lost my job—a delivery person with a freshly broken nose sets a bad image for an establishment."

"What about Foster?" Anything to take my mind off my foot.

"Why would I break his nose for a simple mistake?"

"Didn't he get in trouble for not phoning to confirm the order?"

"He got fired. But he was hired right away by Xiang Lo. Foster lands on his feet. While I was still splinted, the guy I was going with dumped me for a cheerleader with a perfect profile. Listen, I was so depressed that until the swelling went down, I sat up every night watching old movies on TV. I must have seen every flick Vera Hruba Ralston ever made. I know half the dialogue from *One Million B.C.* by heart. You want to hear the last lines from *The Bridge on the River Kwai*?"

I have watched, and cherished, my share of

classic films, but I was not about to encourage any camaraderie with her.

Fauncine came back from the kitchen with an aspirin bottle and a cup of tea. "My father will be here right away."

"No! No! No!" I cried. "Call him back and cancel!"

Fauncine handed me the cup of tea. "They beeped him at the opera, and he had to leave his date. She calls me 'dear heart' and 'sweetie' because she can't remember my name."

Zelma looked wary. "This kid's father is a lawyer?"

Fauncine tossed her the aspirin bottle. "He's an orthopedic surgeon, and he'd never forgive me if her foot is broken."

"Listen," Zelma said to me. "Just so there's no misunderstanding later, why don't I draw up a simple release form for you to sign? You have a computer?"

She was sitting on the floor with pad and pencil when Woodridge arrived, cool and elegant in black tie. Kneeling, he took my foot in his hands. "How did it happen, Iris?"

"She was stomped in some dive roughing up a bimbo who was coming on to her date," Fauncine volunteered.

It took him a minute to regain his professional calm.

I took some stark comfort in the realization

that since he was examining my foot, I was his patient. Professional ethics would certainly preclude his telling my mother how I came to be hurt, especially if I begged him not to.

"We'll go to the hospital," he told me.

Fauncine nodded toward Zelma. "Drop her someplace on the way. I have a feeling that she's behind it all."

"I have my own car," Zelma said with some dignity. "And if you'll just wait until I finish writing up this form—"

"Later," I said.

ARRIVING AT the hospital with your doctor eliminates a lot of red tape. After I was X-rayed and taken back to an examination room, my leg propped on pillows, Woodridge came back and explained my injuries. "You were lucky, but we'll have to keep you off your feet."

"With two kids to take care of?"

"Can't you get your aunt to stay days, too?"

"She's . . . not available days."

"Fauncine would probably be delighted to help." He pulled up a stool and busied himself with my foot. "She admires you enormously."

"She's a good kid." And what a role model I am, I thought.

"I'm giving you a walking cast, but that doesn't mean I want you walking. You'll have to keep the foot up for a couple of days."

After he helped me into his car and stowed the hospital-issue crutches, he turned on the ignition. "I don't think there's any reason for your mother to cut her vacation short. Between Fauncine and your aunt, you'll do just fine. But what are you doing going out with some boy you have to *protect,* Iris? And what kind of a place were you in?"

"A perfectly respectable pool parlor."

He closed his eyes briefly. When he opened them, his voice was stern. "Besides being your doctor, Iris, I know your family. Your father and mother and I went to high school together, remember. As a matter of fact, if things had worked out differently, you might have been my own daughter." He shook his head and started the car.

I was torn between rue, pain, and awe. My own mother had had a scorcher of a doctor pining over her for all these years!

Since I was used to crutches, I got into my house with only a little guiding from him.

With Fauncine hovering over us, he asked, "Where is your aunt?"

"Well, she's . . . she's kind of laid up," I confessed.

"Do you want me to take a look at her?" he offered.

I backed up to an easy chair and lowered myself carefully. "Actually, she's not here. But she only lives a couple of blocks—"

"Not here?" he demanded. "The person who is supposed to be staying with you is not here, and you're getting into untidy brawls at some pool hall? What would your mother say?"

"She would probably say, 'Carpe diem.'" I doubted this profoundly, but I wasn't going to let him get away with any more of this fatherly stuff, and I was feeling a little goofy from the pain medicine they'd given me at the hospital. "She would say, 'You cannot step twice into the same river.'"

"Never pull Latin on a doctor, Iris. And don't try Heracleitis on me, either."

"I could stay over here," Fauncine volunteered. "Then I can feed the kids when they wake. Somebody has to."

Her father hesitated.

Fauncine didn't coax, or sulk, or whine. "We can't drag her poor aunt out of bed to come over here," she pointed out. "And you wouldn't want to wake those little boys and haul them and Iris over to her sick aunt's house. If we leave Iris alone with the kids, how is she going to dress them and feed them in the morning? What will she do if one of them wakes up during the night?"

I was impressed, myself, by her reasoned arguments.

Finally, her father said, "You've made your point . . . points, Fauncine. And this one"—he nodded toward me—"probably should never be left alone at night." Then he reeled off all the standard parental warnings and cautions.

When he left, Fauncine helped me to my room.

I AWOKE AT around nine the next morning with pain in my foot and the sounds of roistering small children in my ears.

My bedroom door opened. Fauncine sidled in, bearing a tray. A tray, yet. She set it down over my lap. The tray had legs! All the days I'd brought my mother meals in bed, I never knew that our tray had legs, nor did my mother so inform me, which must have meant she never knew, either.

The tea was steaming, the brown sugar bubbling on a broiled half grapefruit. "Hey, pancakes!" I said. "I didn't know we had any in the freezer."

"I make them from scratch," Fauncine confided.

I'd seen flour and oil at one time or another in our cupboards. I'd probably seen whatever else went into pancakes. It had just never occurred to me that anyone would put it all together instead of buying frozen.

The boys came tumbling in. Before they could jostle me or my breakfast, Fauncine herded them from my room.

She was a far better cook than my mother, but

then, who wasn't? Nevertheless, I was touched.

Minutes later, Fauncine stepped into my room with a stark announcement. "She's back."

"I'm not signing anything," I warned as Zelma thrust a warped plastic bowl at Fauncine.

"I went to the trouble of making you soup. You could at least be civil." In her scruffy jeans, without makeup, Zelma didn't look that much older than I.

Lifting the lid, Fauncine peered at the soup. "It's purple."

"They had a special on red cabbage."

Fauncine carried the container from the room as if it held some catastrophe of genetic engineering.

Zelma sat on the edge of my bed. "Did I say I was sorry?"

"You did."

"That doctor is a hunk. Forty if he's a day, but what does age matter? And he takes a personal interest, I could tell."

"In my mother, Zelma."

"Funny, he looks much too classy to be a home wrecker."

"My mother," I said coldly, "is a widow. And Doctor Woodridge is divorced."

Nothing abashed this Zelma. "Listen, a doctor in the family is almost as handy as a plumber. And the Bad Seed plainly idolizes you. If ever a kid needed a role model, that Fauncine . . ."

"I don't know if you should go into law, Zelma. Most Mafia dons would probably prefer a more sensitive counselor. Listen, there's something you've got to—"

She set typed papers next to my grapefruit. "Besides, even if he never marries your mother, would a doctor who smolders like Adrian Paul in those *Highlander* reruns send a *bill*? And without a bill, you've got no monetary damages. So you've got nothing coming from this accident. It's too bad you're not old enough to have a regular job, or you'd probably qualify for sick leave."

Merely having her in the room made me feel the need for a storm cellar. "I do odds and ends, Zelma. I mow lawns and wash windows, so I will merely lose hours of honest, remunerative work. What I want you to do—"

As she tried to plump up the pillow I was leaning on, I warded her off.

She held up her hands. "It's probably all for the best. You can use the rest before you get into heavy studying. Believe me, lawsuits are the pits. Being a minor, I couldn't get an attorney to sue anybody over my nose. I live with my sister and her husband, and they refuse to have anything to do with lawyers. I wasn't even eligible for workmen's comp. Since I didn't have health insurance or a doctor with his eye on any of my relatives, I blew my college tuition on a nose job. And Foster Prizer."

I sat up straighter. "Foster?"

"Besides getting fired, he was docked for not calling to confirm those dozen pizzas. He'd just got hired by Xiang Lo when his hearse went on the blink."

"Wait a minute. Wait a minute." I could not help being intrigued. "He was going to deliver pizza in a *hearse*?"

She looked at me as if she were trying to explain calculus to a farm animal. "Come on, Iris. He worked nights, and the buses don't run that late."

"He must have parked it around the corner," I mused.

"What?"

"The hearse. You wouldn't want it in your pizza parlor's parking lot."

"Anyway," she went on, "I loaned Foster the money for the repairs, figuring once he got on his feet, I could always sue him in a small-claims court for my nose. But, again, you have to be eighteen. Meanwhile, Foster's never even paid back the loan. That's why I'm going to be a lawyer. You have to be in a profession where you can take care of yourself."

I might have felt some sympathy for her, if it hadn't been for my foot and her general personality and my mother's car sitting outside a pool hall.

Zelma picked a segment out of my grapefruit and ate it. "So, thanks to Foster, I got a broken nose and lost my job, my fiancé, and my first year's college tuition. He won't answer his door. When I telephone, he changes his voice. When I stake out the pool hall he haunts and attempt to discuss what he owes me, you try to . . ."

"Oh, hell." Fauncine stood in the doorway. "Sign the release."

I did not take the pen Zelma thrust at me. "Would you excuse us for just a moment, Fauncine?"

Alone with Zelma, I seized her wrist. "You bring my mother's car back here before we discuss anything else."

"How?"

"What do you mean, 'How?' "

"So I drive my sister's Datsun to the Pool Hour Resources and bring your car here. How do I get back to the pool hall for the Datsun?"

"Have your sister drive you," I said carefully and clearly.

"She's ticked off that I brought it back last night without putting any gas in."

I tightened my grip. Through my teeth I snarled, "I don't care if you go by balsa raft. *I want my mother's car back here in our garage before high noon.* Clear?"

71

Once she was gone, I tried to rest, but I had too much to think about. With the car back safely, there would be only my foot to explain to my mother. No. No. There would be my foot and why I had not told Aunt Blanche I had a fourteen-year-old staying nights. There would be the emergency money I'd spent on makeup and paid to Fauncine and what I still owed her.

I could hear Fauncine teaching the boys to sing "Stouthearted Men" and other stirring testosterone-laden ballads.

I brooded, swearing to myself I would never again stretch the truth, nor would I abuse it or foreshorten it.

I could at least help Fauncine with Pete and Alvin. As I hobbled into the parlor, the boys came barreling toward me. I managed to sit in the morris chair before they knocked me down.

"Hey! Wow! How did you break your foot?" Pete climbed into my lap.

"Why don't you go back to bed while I fix lunch?" Fauncine suggested.

"I thought I should . . . *oof.*"

"Pete," Fauncine said firmly, "we do not bounce on injured people." She seized my crutch just as Alvin swung it at a table lamp. "If you don't keep your foot up, and it swells more— Alvin, you do not try to ride on her cast!"

"Maybe you're right," I conceded.

After what seemed hours, Zelma returned. She handed me some papers and sat rather carefully on the edge of the bed. "I was going to put your car in your garage, but you didn't tell me Foster's hearse was in residence."

"The hearse!" I whomped my brow with the back of my hand. "We've got to get it out of there!"

"We?"

"Call Foster and tell him to come get it. I don't want my aunt coming over and seeing it."

"He'll change his voice."

"Then you change yours first!"

She tapped her index finger on the papers.

I signed them. "One more thing. Promise you'll think very seriously before you ever apply to law school, Zelma. There's the community to consider. You must have other job skills."

"I write sensitive poetry," she said.

Fauncine brought in a cup of tea on a tray, with one cookie. "I don't know." She glanced at the papers Zelma gathered up. "Signing was either very noble or very dumb."

"Dumb?" Zelma zipped them into her shoulder bag. "A woman who gets her foot stomped over Foster Prizer worries about dumb?"

"Go call him," I told her.

She stood, then hesitated. "I was just thinking," she said.

"Don't," I pleaded. "Don't think, Zelma."

"He loves that hearse," she mused. "Now that we've got it, I could impound it for what he owes me."

"I don't care if you implode it, but I want it off my property first."

"Does it run?" she asked.

"If it ran, would it be in my garage?"

"I don't know." She gazed idly at the posters on my wall. "Foster has a way of making women do crazy things."

Be calm, I adjured myself. Once she's out of the house, she's gone and, in time, will be forgotten. "Zelma, it would cost you hundreds of dollars to have it towed, and I am really not prepared to let you rip off his vehicle."

She ran her fingers over my trophies. "So . . . uh . . . listen. Where's your mother?"

"She is gone on a cruise, a fun-filled adventure, with my cousin, dumping my cousin's kids on me."

"When will she be back?" Zelma seemed to take a real interest in the situation.

"In eight days."

She nodded thoughtfully. "Uh-huh."

"Zelma," I said, "somewhere in that narrow skull, wheels are turning, cogs are grinding. I can tell."

"Well . . . you have kind of a problem."

"I'm getting a feeling," Fauncine pronounced.

"I got your car." Zelma backed toward the doorway. "Only . . . a few odds and ends are missing."

I sat up straighter. *"Odds and ends?"*

She shrugged. "Um . . . hubcaps, radio, window glass. Or didn't it have all those when you parked it there?"

Even with Fauncine restraining me, I managed to lurch out of bed. But Zelma was fast.

The boys ran into the room, big-eyed.

"Out!" Fauncine commanded. "Out, or no dessert with lunch."

They fled.

I dragged myself to the window. Zelma was hastening to her Datsun.

"If you keep yelling, the neighbors are probably going to call the law." Fauncine helped me back to bed. "I'll go check out your car."

She was back in a few minutes, sobered. "You are in deep, deep . . ."

Fauncine had an impeccable memory, a great eye for detail. She even mentioned the flaws the car had had *before* the pool hall.

Lying back on the pillow, I put my arm over my eyes.

"Are you collapsed?" she asked.

"Only emotionally. And if you tell your father or any living soul what has happened, I will—"

She was indignant. "What do you think I am?"

"I think . . . I think I'm very glad you're here."

She grinned fleetingly, then she was all business. "If you hide the car, it won't be so much of a shock to your mother . . . or your aunt. Then you can kind of break it to them gradually."

Shattered as I was, my instinct for self-preservation was reviving. I got myself to the parlor, and Fauncine brought me the telephone.

Foster answered on the third ring. After he assured me that his ribs had only needed to be taped, I said, "I hate to bother you with this, but we have to get Maria out of my garage as soon as possible. If my aunt, who might be at death's door but for garlic—"

"Iris, you believe in *vampires*?"

I was coming to believe strongly in guilt and retribution. "If my aunt, barely recovered, opens that garage door and finds a *hearse* in there, in her condition she might take it for a visitation. This is a woman who believes in alien abductions and miracle creams that cure cellulite."

"I'll be there as soon as I get a ride," he promised.

Fauncine had made corn chowder and tossed green salad.

"What happened to Zelma's soup?" I wondered.

"I tried it on the house plants. You might want to watch out for leaf drop or wilting."

TRUE LOVE MOVES a man, at least when it's for his wheels. He arrived within the hour, which was fortunate, since Pete and Alvin had taken to peering out the window every few minutes with Fauncine.

"He's on an Indian!" Fauncine breathed.

"A what?" I struggled to my feet.

"An Indian. Just merely the greatest motorcycle ever made. A genuine, classic Indian! And he's brought a friend. Oh, wow. What a friend . . ." Her voice trailed off.

I lumbered to the window. I groaned. "Great. Great. Now if my aunt drags herself over here, she'll find our car wrecked, a hearse in our garage, a vintage kick-ass motorcycle in front of our house, Foster with his earring and looks every mother warns her daughter about, and the other . . . the other . . . Oh, wow."

I drew myself up as best I could when Fauncine opened the door.

Foster looked at my foot. A look of consternation, honest consternation, crossed his face. "What happened?"

"Nothing much." Of course I couldn't recount in front of his friend how I got injured attempting to save him from Zelma, hundred-pound Zelma.

"Are you OK?" Foster pressed.

"I'm not ready to talk about it," I said simply. "Foster, you shouldn't jostle your ribs riding a bike."

"They're all taped up. I'll be fine. This is Byron. He gave me a ride over."

Byron. The only Byron I'd ever known was George Gordon, Lord Byron. I knew him well, from the Oxford Standard Authors Series—Byron, who wrote "Don Juan" and "The Destruction of Sennacherib," with those great lines I used to recite in my mind, just for the image and the music:

The Assyrian came down like the wolf on the fold,
And his cohorts were gleaming in purple and gold;
And the sheen of their spears was like stars on the sea,
When the blue wave rolls nightly on deep Galilee.

Now, at my door stood Foster's friend Byron. Six feet four of muscle, bone, and sinew; deep, dark brown eyes; and enough golden hair to stuff a mattress.

This was no lumpen hulk, mind you. This Byron obviously owed his physique to a splendid diet, athletic fields, and some spectacular genes.

George Gordon, Lord Byron, was a scandal in his day, wild and notorious. He probably would have ridden an Indian, and, as I recall, he did sport a great mane of hair.

Foster's friend acknowledged me and the frozen Fauncine with a flash of white, even teeth.

We let him and Foster into the garage through the kitchen. The only thing to do was keep my mind on the problem at hand: to get the hearse out of the garage and my mother's car in. I closed the overhead garage door only partway. If we had to rev the engine, I didn't want us all done in by carbon monoxide. I could only hope any neighbors at home were glued to some tacky talk show.

Maria's lights and windshield wipers worked. Foster and Byron and I looked under the hood. The battery connections were solid, the terminals free of corrosion.

"No room to get another car in here to jump-start her." Foster ran his hands through his hair. He had great hair, long and black and thick. "And we're on a down slope."

Byron's eyes seemed to darken. Was it with the effort of thought? "You'd better not help push, with your ribs all taped. I can—"

"It would be easier," Foster murmured, "if we could get a cable and attach it to Iris's car . . ."

"Foster." I kept my voice mild. "Perhaps you did not take a good look at my car. It was trashed at the pool hall. My car is . . . fragile, at best."

He looked at me as Dr. Woodridge might have. "You left your car in that parking lot?"

I reminded myself that just a day earlier, I'd

thought him the most dazzling male I'd ever met. "I had a little problem with a mashed foot, Foster."

"It wasn't like that when I picked you up."

I was beginning to wonder if male pulchritude and mental prowess were mutually exclusive.

"We can go into this some other time, Foster. Call me quirky. Call me unreasonable. Call a tow truck if that's the only way. But we have to get Maria out of my garage and my car in, soonest."

"Hey, Iris!"

Zelma shoved the garage door all the way up. "Iris, I— *Foster!*"

Before Zelma could reach Foster, he was on his feet and heading for the kitchen. "I'll go find a *Chilton's Manual,* Iris."

"For a fifteen-year-old hearse?" Byron asked.

As I heard my front door open and close, Zelma let the garage door fall. "Foster!" I heard her yell. "You come back here!"

I went back to the engine with Byron. "The distributor and ignition coil are fine," he said, shoving his hair out of his face.

"Air cleaner's new." I looked into the carburetor. "It's clean. Let me open the throttle."

I did, and then we stood together like interns over a challenging patient. "So the air delivery's OK, and she's not flooded," Byron said.

"Let's check the solenoid."

Afterward, we sat on the garage floor while

Fauncine tried to keep Pete and Alvin from climbing all over us.

"It's got to be the starter," Byron pronounced.

I looked up auto parts dealers in the phone book while Byron called them.

"So eighty-five fifty, plus tax, is the cheapest," he said, after the last call.

"Does Foster have that much?"

He shook his head. "I just loaned him a hundred for his pit bull's operation."

I could not help wondering how Foster had borrowed a pit bull. But should I take it upon myself to inform this strapping innocent that Foster would next be borrowing funds to have his Siamese fighting fish neutered? Would I disillusion this splendid youth, threaten a friendship that had begun in the cradle? Would I drive a wedge between Damon and Pythias, wrest Castor from Pollox, split up Achilles and Patroclus?

In a minute. But there was no point in it at this time.

"I could probably raise fifty for the part."

I could not help but note that while Foster had left us, it was Byron who'd stayed to labor over the diagnosis, who was offering to spring for fifty dollars. He might be all brawn and beauty and meager of brain, but his heart was as big as his biceps.

"Let me check some auto dismantlers," he said.

I wondered what the probability was that a local salvage yard might have the one part we needed for this particular model of fifteen-year-old hearse. I was tempted to ask him how many drivers he supposed cracked up their hearses in this town in a year. But I couldn't. That would be like reprimanding a Saint Bernard who was trying to dig you out of an avalanche.

After he left, Fauncine said, "He's going to do it, even if he knows it's almost hopeless. He has to, because he's embarrassed that he doesn't have more than fifty dollars to kick in."

"That's silly," I said.

"He cares what you think about him." She was serious.

I didn't know how to pass this off with a joke, so I got even more serious. "Fauncine, somebody's sure to call my aunt about all the action in my garage. And sooner or later she's going to come over here."

She pondered for only a minute. "We could . . . we could cover your car. We could get some sheets and blankets and secure the ends to the wheels."

"What? And tuck a teddy in with it? And when my aunt asks about the vehicle in front of my house swaddled like—"

"You could say it was just washed."

"Oh, Fauncine, that's weird. That's really weird. I think you may be some kind of genius."

6

THE BOYS STOOD on our front lawn, rapt, as Fauncine and I wrapped.

She had scrounged pieces of rope and clothesline, which we tied to the corners of the bedding, then around the remains of the bumpers.

It is fortunate my mother is at sea, I thought. Anybody watching might be alarmed enough to go looking for her.

Our phone rang, and Fauncine herded the boys ahead of her into the house.

She came to the front door. "My dad wants to talk to you."

I sat on the sofa as she handed me the telephone. "Hi."

"How's the foot?" he asked.

"Oh, hanging in there . . . on there."

"Stay off it, and take the pain pills if you need them—but if one every four hours doesn't help, you have me paged. Let me speak to Fauncine."

She sat on the floor, somewhat more communicative than I'd been. "Sure, Dad. Fine, Dad. Everything's under control. Of course I know you're taking whatsername out tonight. I figured I'd stay here again. Dad . . . *Dad,* it's safer than being home alone. Besides, there's no way she can look after these little boys. Dad, have you ever known me *not* to be careful? I have to fix dinner now. Have a good time. I love you, too."

After the car was wrapped, Fauncine made a casserole and fruit salad with popovers for dinner. Even though my stomach was a churning swamp of terror, remorse, and despair, I could eat. I could even appreciate.

"Your mother must have been a great cook," I said.

"Nah. But Mr. Murphy, my home ec teacher, is." She grinned. "It's kind of nice to cook a meal for somebody who's forced to stay home and eat it." Then she looked a little uncomfortable, as if she'd confided more than she meant to. "I'll pry Pete and Alvin from the TV and take them out back. You can sit on the patio and get some fresh air."

I stretched out on our old webbed plastic

chaise and watched Fauncine and the boys wrestle and roll on the grass.

In that hovering time before twilight, sounds seemed to come from a great distance. It was one of those summer evenings that Tennessee Williams's faded, tragic ladies remember, and remember, evenings where once, somewhere, girls in cotton off-the-shoulder dresses, camellias in their long hair, danced with boys in ice-cream-colored slacks and linen jackets, while the reflection of a full moon shimmered on a lake. The star jasmine tangled on our fence shone white, and the scent of mimosa and honeysuckle was heavy. And all I would remember about this night was the waiting and the worrying. I wondered if Byron ever found a starter. I wondered if he ever found Foster.

When the phone rang, I let Fauncine scramble past me to answer it. It wouldn't be my mother. My mother had probably not given me a thought since embarking on her fling.

"It's your aunt," Fauncine yelled.

Of course it was. It had to be.

By the time I got into the house, Fauncine had brought the phone into the parlor. She put the receiver in my hand and went back out to quiet the boys.

"What is going on there?" Blanche demanded. "I've been getting the most . . . alarming . . . calls from your neighbors. Nobody will say anything concrete, but they're asking me when I'll be well enough to check on you. And the person who answered your phone doesn't even sound as old as you."

"Well, she's . . . she's very mature for her age."

"I'm on my way over."

"Oh, no! No, Aunt Blanche! Your flu!"

"Don't worry about me," she said. "I've been eating garlic day and night."

Not ten minutes later she was at our front door in her old Chanel suit, pale but determined, her hair barely combed.

"What is that all shrouded with bedding outside your house?" she demanded right off.

I reminded myself that I had gotten into this mess by shaving the truth. "Our car."

"Wrapped? Why?"

Before my better self could struggle to the surface, I blurted, "It was just washed."

Convalescent as she was, my aunt could still be intimidating. "What, you're afraid it will catch a chill?"

"She doesn't want it to get all dusty before the wax dries," Fauncine said.

"This is Fauncine," I told my aunt.

"It's been very good of you to keep Iris company, Francine."

"Fauncine," I said.

Blanche looked down at my foot. *"What in the world . . . ?"*

"It got . . . stepped on," I told her.

"You should know that little boys can be rough. We'll have to put ice on it."

"My dad took care of her," Fauncine said mildly, "and ice won't do much good over a cast."

Pete called and Fauncine hurried away.

Stepping closer to me, Blanche silently mouthed, "Who is she?"

"Dr. Woodridge's daughter."

Blanche gazed down upon me sternly. "You have not been honest with me, Iris. And what will your mother say about your having a teenager staying here?"

Fauncine returned, lugging Alvin. "You need a bigger size diaper. He's popping the tabs."

"You can run on home now," Blanche told her. "I need to have a little talk with Iris."

"I can't go home," Fauncine said. "My father will be at a cocktail party and then who knows where until all hours, and we have a temperamental security system."

"What is the world coming to," I asked my aunt, "when parents pursue their own pleasures with no regard for the children they leave to fend for themselves? Is it any wonder kids get into harmless, innocent scrapes, when their own parents offer no guidance—"

"She can stay," my aunt said.

When Blanche went home to pack an overnight bag, Fauncine asked, "Does your aunt work at a trattoria or something?"

"She is eating raw garlic for the flu."

"One thing," Fauncine murmured thoughtfully. "If the flu kills her, they won't have to embalm her."

The phone rang, and she hurried to answer it. She came back carrying it reverently. *"Him."*

"Foster?"

She shook her head. "The big blond Greek god."

"Oh. Him." I took the instrument.

Byron sounded exuberant. "You're not going to believe this, but I scrounged up a starter I think will work. We'll be right over."

"No!" I cried. "Not now!"

There was a silence. Then, "Iris, I thought . . ."

"I'll call when I need you to come, probably tomorrow. It may be on short notice. And we'll have to be prepared to work fast."

I hung up. "Now we have to figure a way to get Aunt Blanche out of the house tomorrow."

The telephone rang again. Fauncine answered, then held the instrument as if it were some decomposing roadkill. "Spider-Woman."

I shook my head.

Fauncine nudged my arm with the receiver. "Maybe she wants to make amends. Somewhere under that exterior, there might even be . . . an interior."

"Fat chance," I muttered.

Zelma sounded as chummy as if she'd never fled me or chased Foster from my garage. "Iris? Listen, I've got a deal for you. There's this woman, Arlene Downing. My sister used to do her nails, and I've sat for her. Anyway, she needs me to meet a plane that gets in a little after midnight. I'll want to park at the curb, so I need you to sit behind the wheel while I rush in to the terminal. I don't want to be walking around the parking areas alone at that hour."

"Why not? They only drive stakes through the hearts of your kind in the daytime."

She barely paused. "Also, I'll feel better having you along in case your car breaks down or anything."

"My car? *My* car?"

"My sister's still ticked off. Besides, I need somebody . . . impressive . . . to come along."

"Tall. You're saying tall."

"I mean, nobody's apt to mess with a woman who looks as if she could deck him."

"Why would we be meeting the plane?" I asked cautiously.

"To pick up a passenger."

"This passenger can't take a taxi?"

"We are talking about a three-year-old," she said patiently.

"Who would be sending a three-year-old alone on a plane at that hour?" I demanded.

"Arlene Downing is paying fifty bucks, of which I will give you twenty percent. That would almost replace the side mirror."

It was the first deep breath I'd taken in hours. "Fifty percent."

"Hey! Out of the goodness of my heart I am offering—"

"Fifty percent or no deal."

She grunted an assent. "You know anybody who can pick me up? I don't have bus fare."

"Did you ever catch up to Foster?"

"Lost him at the corner."

"I'll call him and see if he can get Byron. Give me your number."

"Just say I'm spending the night at your house. If Foster thinks that I'm making any money, it'll be that much harder to put the arm on him."

It occurred to me that Byron might think I was erratic, but I telephoned Foster. "Could you ask Byron to do me another favor?"

"You want to explain?" Fauncine asked when I hung up.

"Not really." But I did.

"You could have just asked for Byron to meet the plane with her," she suggested.

"And pick up a three-year-old on a motor-cycle? Or did you think I'd let Zelma take my car anywhere without me in it and with somebody who looks like a combination of a biker, Michelangelo sculpture, and Chippendale dancer?"

AUNT BLANCHE returned. "I'm feeling a little . . . languorous. This herbal cough syrup has a kick like a mule. I'll get the boys put to bed—"

"No need," I said. "Why don't you just turn in. Fauncine and I will take care of everything."

We put the boys in one of the twin beds in my room. "You sleep in the other," I told Fauncine. "That way, I won't disturb anybody when I come home . . . and if my aunt should get up in the night, she'll think I'm in bed."

As soon as we heard a steady snoring from my mother's room, I said, "Time to undress the car."

The night was beginning to cool. There was a crescent moon, and only a few house lights on down the block.

We didn't dare use a flashlight, for fear somebody might think we were vandals or maybe disciples of the performance artist Christo.

Here I was, old Iris, absolutely trustworthy Iris, Iris of such sterling character my cousin left her only children in my care without a qualm. Iris Hoving, student, athlete, philosophy buff. In two nights, what had I accomplished?

I'd deceived Aunt Blanche and the physician who wanted to be like a father to me.

I had got my foot stomped in a pool hall

brouhaha over a pizzeria renegade. I had left my mother's car to be half stripped outside the same pool hall.

And I was about to plunge even deeper into the morass.

"I don't want you ever to get mixed up in anything like this again," I warned Fauncine.

"I know. But we can't back out now."

I would have adopted her as a sister in a minute, once I'd reformed my ways.

When we finished, we sat on the front porch in the dark, waiting.

It was ten-thirty when I head the throaty roar of the Indian, then silence. I saw shadows approach. Then, under the corner streetlight, I saw the towering figure turn and walk the bike away.

The smaller figure hurried the last quarter block to my house.

Zelma was wearing black sneakers, black jeans, a black shirt, black denim jacket, and a businesslike demeanor.

"You forgot your Ninja scarf," Fauncine greeted her.

Zelma opened the door of the car. "Show time."

AS WE PEELED AWAY from the curb, I hung on to the armrest with both hands. "Leave some tread on the tires!"

"Doesn't shift like a Datsun," Zelma said.

A few miles later, I observed, "We're heading away from the airport."

"We have to stop at Arlene Downing's for our briefing."

"Zelma, we have to be at the airport by midnight!" I protested.

"One."

"You said a little after twelve," I reminded her.

She was unruffled. "One is a little after."

———

ARLENE DOWNING lived in a soaring building girdled with French doors and wide verandas, fronted by a lawn the size of a city park. Limping into the foyer, I couldn't help reflecting that it might have been more reassuring to our client if we'd left me downstairs in the car. But, knowing Zelma, I figured she might be going for a sympathy gratuity.

I wore one canvas sneaker and a fairly new T-shirt. The lower left leg of my loose jeans was split. All in all, Zelma and I looked more like we were going to blow up a power plant than meet a kid at the airport.

The concierge looked up in some alarm as we entered, rising to his feet.

"Ms. Downing," Zelma said loftily, "is expecting us."

He held out one hand as if to block us as he scanned a list.

"She is." He seemed dismayed. "You can . . . go up."

Arlene Downing lived in a penthouse apartment. Her parlor was full of rosewood antiques and marble statues and oil paintings, with a grand piano in one corner. The carpeting was off-white, so deep you would never find a contact lens in it.

Arlene herself was about forty, a little chunky, with a round face. She wore enormous dark glasses.

"You don't know how much I appreciate this," she told us warmly. "I Just can't believe Erik could be so heartless. He fought tooth and nail to get custody of Trevor. He was outraged that he got him for only a month in summer and a month in winter. He drove all the way here to get him, and now, ten days later, he calls me from the Charleston airport to say he's putting Trevor on the plane, just shipping him back to arrive in the middle of the night. I wonder if *she* had something to do with it. After fifteen years of marriage, Erik dumps me for a twenty-year-old, and now it may be that she can't even tolerate poor Trevor."

She took a deep, unsteady breath and handed Zelma a sheet of paper. "He'll be coming in on United. Here's the flight number, my signed note and ID, and the code word to claim him. I'll wait up."

"Boy," Zelma said as we rode down in the elevator. "You could get disillusioned doing this."

"That poor woman. You saw the dark glasses. She must have been crying for hours."

"She just had an eye operation for nearsightedness. That's why she can't go meet the plane."

That seemed especially poignant to me. "Probably did it because Erik wrecked all her self-esteem."

Zelma actually seemed sobered. "It scares you

to see what happens to some couples. I can iden-
tify with Arlene. I haven't had a lot of luck in
picking men. Except for the one who dropped
me, I've always leaned toward colorful but not
truly stable types, like guys that send poison-pen
notes to their own shrinks or take their dates to
survivalist training seminars."

"How about Trevor?" I grabbed for the rail
as the elevator stopped. "Erik leaves him with
Arlene, then takes him from her, and now sends
him back."

I made it across that expanse of marble foyer
without a slip of the crutch, and out to the
Chevy.

"Doesn't Erik know what rejection can do to
a kid? Zelma, could you at least open the car
door for me?"

I slid into the passenger seat and leaned over
to unlock her door for her. "You know how a
trauma like that can affect you when you're
young?"

"Ah, you live through it." Zelma put my
mother's car into gear and we pulled away, leaving only a fugitive stench of burning rubber.
"My father walked out on us when I was five.
When I was twelve, my mother married this
man . . ." She shook her head. Her voice was
low and flat. "He was always getting fired, always coming home looking to fight, always playing the heavy father, with the heavy hand. I

battled that guy steady for four years. Finally, I told my mother I would not have him hit me one more time. So . . . so she sent me to live with my sister. And I survived."

I was embarrassed. Maybe I'd thought a person like Zelma is just born tough and mouthy. It had never occurred to me to wonder about her history.

My mother would never give me up. For a vacation, maybe. But not permanently, and certainly not for a man.

We drove on in silence.

After several miles, it occurred to me that we should have gotten onto a freeway some time back. "Have you ever driven to the airport before, Zelma?"

"Not driven, no."

I felt a prickling on the old cranium. "But you know the way?"

"Everybody knows where it is."

A few minutes later, she asked, "Do you have a map in the car?"

I could not ignore the icy suspicion that had seized me. "Why should I have a map? How could I have a map? The glove compartment door is gone. The glove compartment has been emptied."

We drove on, again in silence, and in darkness, except for the beam from my headlamps and a feeble glow from the occasional functioning streetlight. The skeletons of ruined buildings stood stark and black on debris-littered lots. Now and then a low shadowy figure, a feral cat or dog or monumental rat, scuttled among the desolation.

Zelma spoke. "How hard can it be to find an airport, anyway?"

I felt a throbbing in my temples. "You are telling me you set off to reclaim a child from the airport without plotting your route, without even looking it up on a map? If this is the way you run your life, I can only wonder how many times you've walked into the side of a bus."

"We can ask directions," she said.

"Zelma, it is near midnight. In a neighborhood where the X-rated movie houses and leather bars are closed, with steel shutters pulled down, two women do not accost strangers."

A couple of blocks later, she said, "Here we go."

It was an open bail bond emporium. Through its glass front I saw what looked like the losers of an urban guerrilla skirmish, a few of them bleeding.

"Drive on," I advised.

Instead, she stopped. "If I don't get directions, we could be circling around here all night." She stepped out of the car. "Better lock your door."

I locked my door, telling myself that with the

street so dark, maybe nobody would notice I had no window.

I kept my eye on Zelma as she entered the bail bond place.

So did the urban terrorists.

If one of them so much as twitches, I promised myself, I am leaning on this horn. And if I ever get my mother back—after her car's repaired— I will never, never resent a thing she does for the rest of my life. I will never harbor a grudge. I will never . . .

Zelma walked briskly to the car, waving back at scarred warriors with purple Mohawks, shaved skulls, pierced noses, and tattooed cheeks.

SHE GOT US TO our destination, I'll say that for her. Two wrong exits, a few miles of backtracking, and fifty-three minutes later we were at the road that led directly to the airport.

"I don't remember reading that they were remodeling, do you?" The interesting thing about Zelma was how calm—insouciant is the word— how insouciant she was when anybody else would be frothing. "Read me the signs while I try to figure out where we're going."

I read her the signs:

"Detour!"

"Do not enter! Zelma, *do not enter!*"

"GO BACK! YOU ARE GOING THE WRONG WAY!"

Finally, somehow, we found ourselves rolling up to the United terminal.

"Time is it?" she asked.

"It is twelve fifty-eight, Zelma, and I have aged a lifetime."

"Lucky we left early." She slowed the car. "Look at that. Not a free space at the curb. Not even a five-minute parking space. At this hour, can you imagine?"

"We'll have to park in the garage and walk back."

"Are you out of your mind? Walk through that mausoleum alone at this hour?" She pronounced it "mazoleum," as in "linoleum." "What kind of protection would you be?" she demanded. "Sitting in the car, you're better than nobody, but limping along with your foot in a cast, you'd only attract attention."

Just ahead of us, a bus pulled away from the sidewalk.

Ignoring the red-painted curb, the NO PARK-ING and BUS ONLY signs, Zelma nosed my mother's car right up to the bus stop, with most of the front end sticking into the pedestrian crosswalk.

"No," I said. "You cannot do this. Zelma, you can't even stop here!"

"Scritch over behind the wheel. If anybody says anything, tell him I ran in to pick up the surgeon from Paris who's here for your foot."

Before I could grab her, she scrambled out and dashed into the terminal.

What could I do? I slid behind the wheel, my left foot angled out to the side, and felt for the lever to move the seat back.

Behind me and to my left, someone was honking. I glanced in the rearview mirror.

A bus was bearing down on me, the driver pummeling the horn.

I groped for the ignition.

Zelma had taken the keys.

A man driving a public conveyance should have some control over his temper. I tried to look as if I could not hear him bellowing as he pulled up beside me. Passengers got off the bus, glaring and yelling at me. As they edged between my front bumper and the taxi parked at the cabstand on the other side of the crosswalk, some of them punched my car's hood.

I tried to look as if I were merely occupying the vehicle but in no way related to it, as if I were oblivious to all the threats and hostility.

Inside, I was aspic.

What if the police showed up? Regardless of whether anybody was in it, wouldn't they consider a car parked if it was sitting in a bus zone with no keys in the ignition?

I had to get the engine started and circle around until Zelma came out with Trevor.

How?

I should have left her with the car and dragged myself in for the kid, I thought. Let *her* sit here with a bus driver yelling abuse, with his passengers threatening mayhem.

What would Zelma do then?

Exactly.

A second bus pulled up behind the first.

I clambered out of the Chevy and lifted the hood, supporting myself with one hand on the front fender. If it looked as if the car had stalled, I might buy a few minutes . . . or droplets of mercy.

At this hour, there were few people around. The great overhead fluorescents exending from the terminal to the curb washed the scene in a cold film noir light.

The driver got out of the taxi ahead of me and came stalking to my side. "It's bad enough you park in a bus zone, ma'am, with your nose in the crosswalk. But to stall your engine . . ." He looked at me more closely. "What do you think you're doing, kid? And whose car is this, anyway?"

I slammed the hood shut. It was a pure, instinctive, mindless guilt reaction.

The bus stopped beside me pulled away, the driver red-faced, and another bus pulled up. The driver yelled a few ugly things at us and then pulled up at the curb right ahead of the cab.

A dozen or so people were coming out of the terminal building, but Zelma was not among them. A redcap followed by a tall man and woman trundled a laden cart toward the taxi in front of me. "Got a fare, Mac," he told the driver.

"You're going to have to back this heap out of the way," the cabbie advised me. "I can't get that luggage in the trunk until you do."

The redcap stopped at the curb, gauging the space between the Chevy's front bumper and the taxi's rear.

Mac hurried to open the back door of the taxi on the curb side. In this day and age, I knew, a cabbie opened a door only for royalty or rock stars.

They definitely weren't rock stars. The man was about thirty, with a lean face, a hundred-dollar haircut, and a suit that must have cost more than my mother's vehicle in its prime.

The woman with him was about his age, dressed all in pale gray—shoes, hose, suit. She walked like a model, leading with the pelvis.

From their bearing, it was clear that even if they weren't royalty, they were used to royal treatment.

Even in the charnel-house lighting from the fluorescent overheads, they looked great, cool and unhurried, occupying a different world from the passengers lined up to wrestle their own luggage aboard the bus.

The woman ignored Mac, who stood holding the door open. "I want the pullman and the weekender placed flat, with my cosmetic case on the top," she instructed the redcap. "And be sure they don't rub against one another."

"Just as soon as there's enough space between that car and my trunk to get your luggage in," Mac said.

She addressed the man with her. "Duncan, make that person back up her car."

The cabdriver stepped to my side again. "Kid," he growled, "you are pushing my patience."

I heard the howling then.

Wild, eerie, almost unearthly, that sound belonged on the moors or in a ghoul movie, not at the United Airlines terminal.

The hair on my nape stirred in responsive horripilation.

Hauling on a leash, Zelma lurched out from the terminal. Attached to the leash was sixty or seventy pounds of slavering, bounding, grinning black-and-white Dalmatian.

"Heel, Trevor!" she commanded.

Howling, baying, Trevor dragged her past the redcap and the tall man, the woman and the cabdriver. He brushed them as they leaped out of his way, but he didn't acknowledge them.

This animal was quick to pick his friends. With Zelma dragging behind him like Spartacus to the slave auction, he leaped on me, pinning me against the Chevy.

"Heel! Sit! Stay!" Bracing my hand against the hood, I tried to avert my face, but Trevor got me, hairline to jaw, with a tongue that felt like a warm slab of undrained tofu.

"Not a dog! Not now!" For all his exasperation, the cabdriver sounded almost plaintive. "Time is money, ladies! Get that Hound from Hell into your vehicle and get the . . . Just get out of here!"

Another taxi shot around us and edged in front of the bus that was still parked ahead of Mac in a cab zone. The bus was idling, so that I was beginning to feel like a repository for noxious fumes.

Zelma handed me the leash. "Hold him while I pull around the cab."

"Hold him?" I was barely maintaining myself in an upright position. Looping Trevor's leash around my arm, I groped back toward the passenger door. "Heel, boy."

He planted his front paws more firmly on my shoulders, slurping my face vigorously.

I sank, Trevor with me, until I was squatting on the sidewalk, balancing with my cast out in front of me and between the dog's legs. "Zelma, just back up the car."

She got behind the wheel of the Chevy, the redcap lifted the pullman case from the cart, and the woman in gray began to step into the taxi.

Zelma started the engine, and the car lurched forward, into the rear of the cab.

As the woman in gray screamed, the dog cringed, tail glued to his belly, chest pressing my bad foot into the pavement. Trembling, he lifted his head and bayed a long, wild response.

Duncan rushed to the woman. "Are you all right, Lorelei?"

Zelma sat, pale, gripping the wheel. "It doesn't shift like a Datsun."

A vein in his right temple engorged and throbbing, the cabdriver strode back to lean in her window. "You and me acquainted?"

I had never seen Zelma at a loss for words before. She only shook her head.

"So this is just random violence you're into," he growled, "*Thelma and Louise* stuff, nothing personal."

Lorelei stalked back to Mac. "Even if she's not drunk, she's too dangerous to be driving."

It had to happen. I was only surprised that it hadn't happened sooner. A police cruiser stopped behind my car. An officer got out, hand on her baton, and strolled toward us in that deliberate way police walk. "Trouble?"

I tried to look as if I were just sitting with a dog in an inconvenient place.

"Trouble?" Lorelei peered at the name strip on the officer's shirt. "I would say so, Ms. Bradley." She nodded toward Zelma. "She almost killed me."

"Let's get everybody on the sidewalk and out of the traffic lanes." Once she'd collected everyone but Zelma on the other side of my car, Bradley asked, "Is anyone injured?"

Duncan, Zelma, Mac, even the redcap assured her they were unhurt.

"I will have to see my doctor to determine that," Lorelei said.

"Are you aware of anything that might be an injury?" This was one professional cop. "Would you like me to call for medical assistance?"

"Come off it, Lorelei," Duncan said. "You were barely jostled."

She glared at him. "I'm all right. But that doesn't excuse what happened."

Bradley looked down at my foot. "You're not by chance in the business of pretending to be injured and then suing—"

"Oh, no. Never." I hitched closer to my car and groped my way to a standing position, leash loose around my arm, Trevor close beside me.

"I need to see your driver's license," Bradley told Zelma.

Through the open passenger side window, Zelma handed her a card.

Bradley glanced at it. "All right. Now your vehicle registration and proof of insurance."

Zelma gazed at me mutely.

I could only stare at the empty glove compartment.

Zelma flipped both visors down. There was nothing attached to them. She patted over the floor mats.

Could my mother have taken the registration slip and insurance card with her? No. She'd want Blanche to have them in an emergency. Were they with my aunt? In a desk drawer at home? In the steel box under my mother's bed?

Zelma looked on the backseat. She looked under both front seats.

Don't panic, I told myself fiercely. Bail was invented for situations like this.

I pictured my aunt out looking for a bail bond place at two in the morning. Never. Never. I could never send my mother's only sister out on the streets at that hour, in those neighborhoods.

Fauncine would take it as her personal responsibility—or quest—to spring me. She'd have to call her father.

Before I'd let him know, I would spend the night in the slammer along with the flotsam of society. But I could not take shelter there forever.

And what of the dog, the poor dog? What of Arlene Downing, waiting for us to deliver him? What of the fee we had not collected in advance?

"How long do we stand here while they play games with you?" Lorelei asked Bradley.

I should have let Zelma drag Foster out of the Pool Hour Resources by his bola. I should have never interceded.

OK, say I interceded. I should have crawled home rather than get any more involved with Zelma.

Trevor looked up at me, whining.

"It's OK, boy." I was reduced, finally, to lying to a dog.

The officer bent to speak to Zelma. "You are aware that your registration and proof of insurance are to be kept with your vehicle at all times?"

"It's not my vehicle," she said.

Lorelei threw up one hand, vindicated. "I knew it."

Trevor whined, his tail still low.

"Step out on this side, please," Bradley told Zelma.

"Wait a minute. Wait a minute. What's this?" Zelma felt between the driver's seat and the shift console.

"Back out, and keep your hands where I can see them!" Bradley told her crisply.

Holding two slips of paper between the first fingers of her raised right hand, Zelma backed out of the Chevy.

"Hand me those papers, very slowly," the officer instructed Zelma.

Bradley examined the slips. "Registration, current; proof of insurance, current." She looked at Zelma. "Who is Dolores Hoving?"

"My mom," I whispered.

"Let me see your driver's license," Bradley told me.

I groped in my shirt pocket and handed her my learner's permit.

She glanced at it. "Does your mother know you have her car?"

"Well, she's . . . she's away on vacation," I stammered.

The officer's voice was cool. "So you're out joyriding?"

"Not joyriding!" I tried to get my cast out from under Trevor's front paw. "We had to come pick up . . . the dog."

"You stay right where you are," the officer told Zelma and me. "Do not move a muscle, either of you."

We stood quite still while Bradley went back to the cruiser and spoke on her radio.

She strode back to us.

"Why are we standing here? Why are you not running them both in?" Lorelei demanded.

"They can't just leave the dog," Duncan pointed out.

Lorelei was implacable. "They can call somebody to come impound the thing."

"The car's clean, and so are both of you," Bradley told Zelma and me. "But you're still parked in a red zone, halfway into a crosswalk, and you rear-ended a taxi." She took out a pad.

"OK," Mac began his statement before she asked him a thing. "This car is parked in the bus zone, nosing into the passenger walk, right? The tall kid has the hood raised. I offer to help her, since she has traffic backed up. The redcap comes out with these two people, and we can't get their luggage to my trunk. Then the shorter kid comes out with the dog and gets behind the wheel and rams my cab."

"It doesn't shift like a Datsun," Zelma confided.

"Go ahead and exchange information." Bradley handed Mac my insurance card.

He bent and examined his bumper as best he could. "It looked the same before." He stood up and looked at Bradley. "I don't want to get the kid in any more trouble."

I sucked my lips in between my teeth so I wouldn't sob.

Trevor was one sensitive, sympathetic dog. His flanks trembled. He kissed my hands.

"If you don't need anything more from us," Duncan told the officer, "I'd like to get going. We've had a long flight."

"You are *not* going to simply release those

two!" Lorelei smacked the side of my Chevy. "I happen to know a few people in the mayor's office . . ."

Trevor lifted his leg.

"No!" I flung myself in front of Lorelei.

Almost in time.

Duncan bent and helped me to my feet . . . foot. "Are you all right?"

Lorelei stared at Trevor. As she regarded my soaking jeans and her own barely sprinkled skirt, her voice dropped an octave and many, many decibels. "That was meant for me!"

"I've heard of taking a bullet for somebody," the cabbie muttered in awe, "but never . . ."

Zelma looked shocked, almost convincingly shocked. "I have never, ever seen him do anything like that."

Officer Bradley seemed to recognize that this was a situation for which she had no protocol, no precedents. "Let's just get everybody out of here. You kids, I'm letting you off with a warning." She impaled me with a gaze that would have made my aunt Blanche freeze. "But if I ever catch you taking your mother's car without her permission . . ."

"You are just going to ignore that . . . that animal's assault?" Far from being dampened, Lorelei's rage seemed more inflamed.

"I'm not sure how we would write it up." Bradley's voice was bland, but there was a look in her eyes that made me suspect she was having a hard time keeping a professional attitude. "I don't think there's anything in the penal . . . Never mind."

Lorelei was trembling. "I *demand*—"

"It's very late," the officer told her. "It's a busy night, and I have hours of crime and violence yet to contend with." She turned to me. "Just get that dog in your car and go home, and thank heaven that I remember that I was once your age."

"Law enforcement," Lorelei murmured in a tone of deadly contempt. But she let Duncan lead her to the taxi.

"Thank you!" I told Mac.

"Just hang on to that dog." He handed me my insurance card, then hurried after his fares.

As Officer Bradley strode back to the cruiser, her shoulders seemed to be shaking.

Her arms around Trevor's middle, Zelma boosted his front end, then his rear, onto the backseat.

ZELMA REMEMBERED the route back to Arlene's pretty well.

I only had to coach her a bit. "Wrong way, Zelma! *Do Not Enter* means DO . . . NOT . . . ENTER!"

His chin resting on my shoulder, the dog drooled on my ear.

"I never saw anything like the way you got between him and that woman," Zelma said. "Not since Joan Crawford threw herself between the bullet and the man she loved in *Johnny Guitar*."

My jeans were plastered, cold and wet, to my thighs.

As Zelma groped for the heater, I warned, "Don't. It will bring out the aroma." I shoved Trevor's nose out of my ear. "You did not tell me, Zelma, that we were picking up an animal. Nobody told me that Trevor was a dog."

"You never asked. And I didn't know how you'd feel about fur on your upholstery."

"It beats dog pee."

"You have a lot of hostility in you, Iris."

"I know it takes a tacky person to hold a grudge against woman's best friend. But sitting in wet, reeking jeans and soggy shoes kind of curdles the milk of human kindness."

"You want to go back to the terminal and change?"

"No. No. I would not navigate another cloverleaf with you if we were escaping a tsunami. I would not leave you alone behind the wheel of my mother's car. And what did you mean, 'I have never, ever seen him do anything like that'? For all you know, it is his wont."

"You don't suppose that's why he got sent back here so soon?" she mused, easing into the fast lane of the freeway. "I wonder if he had a personality clash with Erik's new friend and expressed it . . . that way?"

Not even a perfunctory grovel from either of them.

Trevor sat behind me, grinning, panting, his breath humidifying my neck.

"I was crazy," I said.

She shrugged. "Everybody's crazy now and then. That's my theory."

I hated to compromise my indignation by agreeing with her, but her explanation was the only one that made sense. "I went out with Foster and took my mother's car because I happened to be temporarily insane at the moment. I let you drive me home after you mashed my instep because my cerebrum was off-line. But that's not enough. No. Before, I only had my foot smashed and my mother's car stripped. I let you talk me into this because I was prime for confinement. And now I am dealing with a traffic accident, police citations—"

"She didn't give us a citation."

"She could have."

"But she didn't. If there'd been a citation, she would have had us sign it and handed us a copy."

Obfuscation. Besides a whole repertoire of attitudes, she had mastered obfuscation.

I went back to dwelling on the obvious. "No woman in her right mind would go out with Foster."

"I never did."

I held tight to the armrest, reminding myself that any sudden move in her direction might distract her from driving. But I was so overwhelmed with what I'd brought down on myself, it drowned out everything, even righteous outrage. "I thought going out with Foster Prizer would be . . . What's the Spanish warning? 'Be careful what you wish for. You might get it.' "

"That is dire," Zelma conceded.

"There's also a Spanish proverb:

The sins you do
by two and two,
you pay for one by one."

"I don't get it," she said.

I shoved the dog, who was attempting to climb between us, into the backseat again. "What do you mean, you don't get it?"

"Does it mean the sins you do by two and two, as in two people doing them, or the sins you do by two *and* two as in one person doing two sins at a time?"

"You do not analyze a proverb!" I snapped. "It's poignant. That's what it's supposed to be— poignant."

As we sped through the night, I imagined my

cousin Ellie standing at the ship's rail in the moonlight, an ocean breeze playing with her hair, the purser or maybe even the captain plying her with champagne.

It's hard to sustain a fantasy when you have a large Dalmatian snuffling in your ear and an acrid ammonia aroma rising from your jeans.

WE ARRIVED at Arlene Downing's apartment building at three.

Trevor knew the place. Baying, howling, he scrambled to climb over me out of the car.

I followed after him and Zelma. "How do we get him up to Arlene?"

"In the elevator."

"They allow dogs in the elevator?"

"You think somebody walks him down six flights and then up every time he has to go?"

The concierge was nowhere to be seen.

Trevor bounded into the elevator, dragging Zelma.

I limped after with my crutch.

"Look." I nodded toward the sign posted right

over the buttons. NO PETS. ANIMALS MUST USE
FREIGHT ELEVATOR.

"Must be new," she said.

IT WAS ONE OF the most touching reunions I have
ever beheld. Arlene fell to her knees, throwing
out her arms as the dog flung himself at her.
They cried. They kissed.

Arlene looked up at us, her arms around Trevor's neck. "Thank you! I hope he wasn't any
trouble." Then she got a glimpse, or maybe a
whiff, of my jeans. "Did he do that?"

"He did," I confirmed.

"I'm so sorry. He tends to have such an ex-
pressive bladder." Arlene stood, and with the
dog chewing at her ankles, managed to open a
purse that was on the foyer table and to take out
a twenty-dollar bill. "Please take this, with Trevor's regrets."

I took it, though I could see no inkling of
regret in the dog. He was wagging his whole
rear end.

She took a check from her purse. "Be sure you
hold this until Monday. It won't be good until
then."

I might have been supported by a crutch, but
I was taller than Zelma, with a longer reach.

Arlene thanked us a couple of more times, and
then we left.

"What a reunion," I said in the elevator.

"Right up there with Warren Beatty and Diane Keaton in *Reds*." With the check in my hand, I was beginning to feel—dare I say it?—wild and sardonic.

Zelma reached for the check. "I can cash it Monday. You've been on your feet too much already."

I held on to it. "Don't worry about me, Zelma. I figure, if I have the check, I won't have to look you up for my share." I glanced at it. "Sixty dollars."

She had no more shame than the dog did. "Imagine that. A tip."

"Splitting the tip, it's thirty each."

"This was my deal I cut you in on!"

I put the check in my shirt pocket.

"What about the twenty she gave you?"

"Fifty dollars won't even scratch the car repairs."

I'll say one thing for Zelma. She's not one to cherish a grudge. We were on the road for only a few minutes when she asked, "Want to stop for nachos?"

"There's a demented streak in you, do you know it? Do you not see, do you not smell, the condition of my clothes?"

"I meant nachos to go."

"I want to shower, Zelma. I want to get out of these jeans. I've got this thing about riding around reeking wet at three A.M."

She drove on. But she was not silent for long. "You know who that cabdriver walked like? James Coburn in *The Magnificent Seven.*"

"Zelma, if you even attempt reciting the last lines from *Bridge on the River Kwai,* you may have to hunt me down for your thirty dollars."

I DIDN'T HAVE the energy to rewrap the Chevy. We parked around the corner from my house. The streets were dark and silent, and I felt tired and heavy. Walking with a cast and a crutch at the end of a challenging day was hard work.

Zelma followed me into the kitchen. I tossed the car keys on the counter by the sink and poured a glass of juice for each of us. "There's the phone."

"What for?"

"To call yourself a cab."

"Call a cab? I don't have a penny!"

"OK. I'll loan you the twenty, but I want change back."

"If I go home now, I might wake up my sister and her husband."

"Zelma, if they wake up and find you gone, they'll be frantic."

"No," she said. Her voice was quiet and flat again, and she didn't look at me. "They will be ticked off if I wake them, but they won't be worried if I'm gone."

That went through me. That went right through me.

I remembered the lines in Springsteen's "Born in the U.S.A." about being beat so much you spend your life covering up.

Maybe all that flash, all that fast talk—all that was Zelma's covering up. But you don't tell somebody like this that you understand until you've been friends a long, long time.

"OK," I said. "The sofa's too short for me, anyway. I'll take the floor. But you have to get up before dawn to help me dress the car."

I went into the bathroom to peel off my jeans and wash.

WHEN I WOKE, it was daylight, and I was alone in the parlor. I stumped into the kitchen, where Fauncine was bustling around.

"Zelma's gone?"

"She's helping the kids dress. She got up early to swaddle the car."

I looked out the window. The Chevy was at the curb, all shrouded.

"Did she tell you about last night?" I asked.

"More or less."

"Probably less."

From our cupboards Fauncine got out foodstuffs I didn't even know we had.

I managed to sit on a kitchen chair. "It may

take me awhile to pay you all that I owe you, Fauncine."

"Worry about fixing your mom's car," she said.

"I'm holding a check for sixty dollars that will be good Monday. I can give you twenty cash today."

She tucked a dish towel into the waistband of her jeans for an apron. "Sixty dollars probably won't even cover your insurance deductible," she said.

"No. No . . . we couldn't afford comprehensive coverage."

"Oh, wow."

"Fauncine," I asked, "have you ever done anything that kept snowballing into a catastrophe like this?"

"I'm only fourteen," she protested.

My forehead felt hot and my hands cold.

"What I would do . . . ," Fauncine said slowly. "What I would do is ask myself what Zelma would do."

I sat up straighter, the better to assure myself that I'd not lost my senses, that I was not hallucinating the voice of Zelma herself.

Fauncine was calm. Fauncine was implacable. "You notice that you're in deep trouble, and Zelma isn't. I just wonder if maybe Zelma is smarter than you in certain ways. Only a few ways. That count."

Zelma came into the kitchen looking rested and unworried, herding Pete and Alvin, all dressed and combed. "Shouldn't we wake your aunt for breakfast?" she asked me.

"My aunt goes better with pasta and a nice red wine."

The boys were a little boisterous as we sat down, but Zelma quelled them with a glance.

... *What I would do is ask myself what Zelma would do.* ...

She seated herself as if she'd been around my house for years. "What are these?"

"Scones," Fauncine told her.

"Stones?" Pete demanded.

"Scones." Fauncine buttered one and put it on his plate. "From an old Scotch recipe."

The kid trusted her. He took a bite and looked at her with something like reverence. "You must be the greatest cook that ever lived."

"In my age bracket," she assured him modestly.

Zelma ladled jam on a scone, then wolfed down two more and drained a glass of juice.

She had a splendid appetite. And why wouldn't she?

... *You notice that you're in deep trouble, and Zelma isn't.* ...

Zelma had come out of this mess with thirty dollars, while I still had a wrecked car and a ruined life.

. . . I just wonder if Zelma isn't smarter than you in certain ways . . . that count. . . .

I didn't get to be a top athlete by ignoring a challenge.

I leaned forward, my elbows on the table. "So, Zelma. If it hadn't been for your almost getting us busted, we probably could have picked up Trevor and got back in a couple of hours. That's not bad money, even split evenly."

"It didn't shift . . ." she began.

I raised a hand. "Just commenting. When you consider all the complications we ran into, the wrong turns, the other stuff, plus a fee for use of the car, I think we might consider raising our rates."

For a minute I thought I might have to Heimlich old Zelma. But she seized her cup of tea and drained it like a drought-ravaged wildebeest encountering a Serengeti water hole.

Fauncine hurried to take another batch of scones from the oven.

"I'm talking real money," I went on. "What did you get for delivering pizzas—besides a broken nose? I've got the car and the brains. Fauncine has the organizational skills. And you've got the . . . the . . ."

"Chutzpah." Fauncine had dropped a scone, but I could see she was as delighted as she was surprised to be included.

"Hey!" Zelma glowered at her.

"Leave the kid alone!" I told Zelma. That's my favorite line from *The Wanderers*. Now that I had Zelma off balance, I closed in. "This is The American Way. This is how you get ahead in this world. You own your enterprise, you set your hours . . ."

"You deduct all the expenses from your income tax," Fauncine put in.

"You want to spend the rest of your life stalking Foster, begging your sister for the use of her car?" I challenged Zelma. "Don't you want to go back to school before it's too late, before you drift into a life of aimless, menial work?" No point mentioning that I needed money for car repairs. I recalled that old TV deodorant commercial—*Never let them see you sweat.* "I'm thinking a single, dignified ad. Maybe just 'Will Do Anything,' with your phone number."

"Iris!" Zelma protested. For the first time, she seemed at a loss. "My sister's got three kids and one bedroom! She fights with her husband. You want us taking business calls *there*? I mean, that's just one reason why the whole idea is ridiculous."

Fauncine sat at the table again. "The ad could use a little refining. We clarify. 'Will Do Anything Legal, Moral, Ethical . . .'" She snatched the sugar bowl from Pete as he tried to empty it over his brother's head. ". . . and Safe.'"

I reflected for only a moment. "Nah. *Safe* would cut down on a lot of business. Also, *safe* makes us sound like wimps. *Legal, ethical,* and *moral* ought to cover it."

"That depends on your risk tolerance," Fauncine said. "Process serving, I don't know, even after Zelma's eighteen. But courier, personal shopper, gofer, schlepper—"

"Wait a minute!" Zelma broke in. "You insult me, you put me down—how can you think I would be involved in any kind of social or business or even trivial pursuit with you two?"

I didn't waver. "I think in the law it's called recompense, Zelma. If it weren't for you, I'd have two functional feet, an intact car, and the memory of a magical evening with Foster."

She left without even borrowing bus fare.

Fauncine got up to clear the table. "I never realized you had a feral streak in you, Iris."

"Only when pushed to the wall," I said.

AUNT BLANCHE came into the kitchen looking only a trifle pale, and Fauncine immediately set a place for her.

I lingered at the table with them while the boys played in the backyard, but I couldn't help wondering whether Zelma's sister would ask where she'd been all night.

I knew that if my aunt had wakened in the middle of the night and found me gone, she would have had a fit. I should confide in her, I thought guiltily. I should tell her about Foster and my mother's car and the airport and Trevor.

No. It would only make her feel she'd screwed up on chaperoning us.

The telephone rang, and Blanche answered it.

"Hi! How's it going?" She put her hand over the mouthpiece. "It's your mother, Iris."

I hadn't counted on this. I hadn't counted on having a talk with Mom even before she returned, even before I was on my feet, even before I'd begun to get the car fixed.

"You go first," I told my aunt.

"Everything's fine," she assured my mother. "I had a little bout of flu but— No, no, I'm completely over it. No, none of them shows any signs. Trust me; if any of them so much as sniffles, I will— No. No, nobody is sniffling. Everything is under control." She glanced at my cast. "Oh. Except . . ."

I shook my head, beseeching.

Blanche can be quick on the uptake. "Except the weather's been iffy, but it's cleared up. All right." She turned toward the parlor. "Pete! Your mother wants to talk to you. Hello—Ellie? No, nobody has the flu. Yes, I have the pediatrician's number. No, there is no need for you to fly back today. Yes, they're right here."

"Pete!" Blanche's shout was more vigorous. "You get in here and talk to your mother!"

This is known as family values.

Like an aristocrat approaching the guillotine, Pete let Fauncine herd him to the table. Blanche clapped the receiver into his hand and warned, "Don't talk silly."

As Fauncine went to the parlor for Alvin, I told

my aunt, "I don't know why anybody in her right mind would want to talk to anybody his age long-distance. Pure masochism."

"It's maternal instinct," she said.

"Same thing."

Pete conversed with his mother. He said, "Yeah." He said, "No." "Nothing." "I don't know." "All right."

As Fauncine brought Alvin close, Pete dropped the receiver into his hand. Alvin blew into the mouthpiece. Alvin made noises like the burbles of a toxic waste dump. Alvin peered into my aunt's eardrum.

"Well." Blanche wrested the receiver from him. "Put your aunt back on, Ellie." She handed me the phone.

I had no choice. It would seem unnatural if I declined to speak to my own mother. Besides, if she thought I was coming down with something, she might hurry home.

"Hi, sweetheart." Her voice was gentle. "Did you get my postcards yet?"

"You've only been gone four days, Ma."

"So how's everything going, baby?"

"Oh, everything's just . . . going along." How shabby. How sneaky. But how could I tell my own mother everything that had happened and cause her to cut short her vacation and rush home in anxiety and apprehension? My mother needed a vacation. My mother deserved a vacation.

At least until her car was repaired.

My mother was still talking, telling me about the port she was calling from, and shipboard events, and the souvenirs she'd bought for me and Blanche. As a matter of fact, she talked a little too fast, too long, too brightly, like somebody who is feeling guilty.

She should, I thought for a second. If she'd never left, everything would have been OK.

Come on, I told myself. She was to predict all the catastrophes I brought down on myself?

I guess any mother would be alerted by a silent kid. "You're sure everything is all right?" she asked.

"Aunt Blanche is here," I said reassuringly. "And we've been eating very well, and the boys are happy."

"So what have *you* been doing?" she pressed.

"Oh, this and that."

"You're not just staying at home all day, I hope."

"Oh, no. No."

"Good. You still have enough money?"

"I . . . We're eating like gourmets."

"You tell Blanche she's an angel." Her voice dropped, and almost in a whisper she added, "I miss you, baby. I love you and I miss you."

"I . . . I love you, Ma." It's OK for the person who has gone away to say, "I miss you." But if I told her I missed her, it might make her feel even more guilty.

I wanted her to enjoy her vacation.

It would kind of buffer her against what she was coming home to.

AFTER SHE TIDIED the kitchen, Fauncine went out back to watch Ellie's kids. "I'll be in to make lunch," she said.

"There's no need," Blanche remonstrated. "With me here—"

"That's OK. I've got everything planned."

"That child," my aunt observed, when Fauncine had gone outside, "is going to grow up to run a perfect home. Probably the White House. No. More likely an industry, or a nation."

"Yeah. I worry about her. She's *too* responsible for a kid. All that cooking, all that tending to things, trying to get the approval of a father who's wrapped up in his work and his social life."

Blanche stood. "If she's going to be staying around, I might as well run home and pick up my mail and water my plants. Is there anything you need?"

"Nothing." How little she knew.

"If you're sure you're all right, I might drop by the health food store."

"Oh, yes! By all means," I urged her.

"I might be gone three or four hours if I take the bus. I hate to drive somebody else's car."

"I don't *blame* you!" I said warmly. "You should take the bus, take time to . . . oh, to enjoy the day, linger, savor . . ."

The minute my aunt left, I telephoned Foster. "Now!" I told him.

"I'll have to get hold of Byron—"

"Now!" I repeated. "Tell him we have a very narrow window of opportunity here! You probably shouldn't ride that Indian until your ribs are healed."

I'd just hung up when the telephone rang.

It was Woodridge. "How's your foot?" he asked.

"Better. Better." A foot was my most minor concern.

"Is everything all right? Have you heard from your mother? When will your aunt be there?"

"Yes, yes, and in a couple of hours."

"And she's going to spend the night there?"

"Absolutely. Oh, and I want to thank you for everything."

"Good. Let me talk to Fauncine."

Her conversation with him was something like Pete's with his mother:

"Hi, Dad. Fine. Fine. I need to get lunch started. Dad, they *need* me here. OK. I know. I promise. I love you, too."

After she hung up, she told me, "I get to stay until after dinner, then we renegotiate. So when are those guys coming to work on the hearse?"

"Soon, I hope. Soon."

"Iris, do you think I'd look older if I tried some of your makeup?"

"Absolutely not!" I exploded. "Look where that kind of thing got me! You start painting your face, there's no telling where you'll end up."

Fauncine persuaded the boys to take a nap in my mother's room. She could probably run a maximum security institution some day, I reflected.

I heard the roar of a motorcycle approaching.

As Fauncine hurried into the garage to open the overhead door, I hobbled after her.

What is it with my gender? I wondered, as Foster and Byron entered. Here I am, a woman with a certain intellectual strength, and I have trouble taking my eyes off this big blond, who probably thinks the Magna Carta is a large Italian roadster.

"Foster, your poor ribs!" But it was good of him to come. "Shut the overhead door." I was *this* close to getting Maria out and my car in before anybody told my aunt about the comings and goings at my house. There was no point in having these guys on display now.

"We'd have better light with it open," Foster pointed out.

"Consider this a covert operation," I told him.

"Four of us in my garage working over a hearse might pique the neighbors' sense of the bizarre."

"Do you have a trouble light?" Byron asked.

"Let me get a flashlight."

As I pawed through our kitchen junk drawer, one elbow on the counter, I murmured to Fauncine, "Even with the hearse out and the Chevy in, my mother will still be home in a week. There's just no money to get the car fixed."

She put her hand on my shoulder.

"My mother loves that Chevy," I said, "but she doesn't trust machines. She'd be scared to drive it in the shape it's in. I can't help but think of her out there in the slush and sleet, come winter, walking six blocks to the bus stop, shivering, waiting for a bus, all because my hormones overwhelmed my judgment."

When the phone rang, I reached for it. It wouldn't be my mother, who had just spent a fortune long-distance. I didn't much care who else it might be.

"So we'd pay for the ad out of the sixty?" Zelma asked.

I kept my voice casual. "The paper could probably run it the day after tomorrow, and if your sister's a subscriber, they'd bill her, and we could either pay her from the sixty or out of our first job."

Fauncine took the receiver from my hand. "Come over for lunch, and we'll nail down the details."

"WHILE YOU GUYS are working on the hearse," Fauncine said, after I located the flashlight, "I'm going to run home and get a recipe book."

She was going to be fine. She was far from immune to male beauty, but she was barely fourteen. She knew she wasn't up to Foster and Byron speed.

With any luck, I thought, and with me around to keep an eye on her and to remind her that rippling muscles and smoldering gazes all but destroyed my life, she'll avoid my mistakes.

"Your car keys are by the sink," she said, and left by the front door.

I was in the garage when I heard our front door open.

I never would have dreamed I could move so fast on a crutch. I intercepted my aunt before she got to the kitchen. "Aunt Blanche! What are you—?"

"Missed the damn bus. I'd better take the car."

From my mother's bedroom, I heard the sound of fresh young voices raised in brawling.

"Ah, the boys must be up. Aunt Blanche, would you separate them?"

As she hurried out of the kitchen, I stumped through the kitchen and opened the door to the garage. "We've got complications. Could you—?"

I shut the door quickly as I heard Blanche returning and made my way into the parlor.

She came in holding Pete by the hand and Alvin under her arm. "Where's your friend Fauncine?"

"She's neat," Pete declared staunchly.

"Neep," Alvin echoed, in a voice like a bull-frog, the first word I'd ever heard him utter.

"Oh, good heavens." Blanche held him out from her at arm's length. "He's still not house-broken?"

"Go get your brother's diapers," I told Pete.

He came back dragging the toy chest his mother had left. Pulling the lid off, he began hauling toys from it. Alvin went limp, hanging over Blanche's arm, making raspberry noises and drooling down his chin.

"Your teddy!" Pete crooned, holding it over his head.

Struggling free, Alvin threw himself at his brother.

"What do you do with them when they're like this?" Blanche asked me.

"Foist them on Fauncine." I was thinking desperately, trying to construct a strategy.

The boys rolled around on the carpet together, grunting, snarling, shrieking.

"Stop that!" Aunt Blanche commanded.

Kneeling, she tried to hold them apart. "When is she coming back?"

"Fauncine?"

Alvin's soggy diapers slipped down around his ankles, but he kept flailing at his brother.

Through her teeth, my aunt said, "Fauncine. Anyone. With you off your feet, these boys— stop that kicking, Peter!—really need an active young person to relate to. And it will give me a chance to do your laundry. With little Alvin here, I imagine it has reached critical mass. Even the sheets are soggy."

"Fauncine went home for a while." I sat on the sofa and slapped my hand on the coffee table. "Hey!" I told the boys, "Zelma is coming to lunch. If you don't freeze right now, I'm going to tell Zelma!"

Instantly, they went civilized. Silently, Pete fetched the remote. He and Alvin sat before the television while Pete turned it on, found a channel, and even turned the sound down.

"Will this last?" Blanche whispered to me.

"What does?" I asked, bitterness seeping into my voice.

She stood and strode into the kitchen. "I'll take the car and be back—"

I tried to struggle to my feet. "Aunt Blanche, wait!"

"I won't be any time." She scooped the keys off the counter and opened the door to the garage.

My aunt is tough. She didn't even shriek.

Maybe it was her tread or the look on her face. But as she staggered back into the parlor, Pete and Alvin gazed up at her in silence, awed.

In a few long strides, Byron reached her side. His great grimy arm encircled her waist. "That's okay, ma'am. I won't let you fall. Foster, get her a drink."

"I'll do it," I said. "Foster, would you take the boys out back?"

They went with him cheerfully.

As Byron eased her into the morris chair, my aunt fixed her gaze on me. "There is a hearse in your garage."

I suppose anybody, hit by one thing after another after another, would finally just wear out. I was too tired, too defeated, too ashamed, too disgusted with my foul-ups to edit the tale. I told her everything, straight, no excuses, no rationalizing, no glossing over for Byron's ears.

When I finished, Blanche sat quite still. Then she spoke. "Does your mother's car run? Is it safe to drive?"

I nodded.

"I will take it to a body shop and get an off-the-cuff estimate." She stood.

"Aunt Blanche . . ."

She left.

". . . you'll have to undress it," I called out weakly.

"Should I go help her?" Byron asked.

I could only nod.

When he came back, laden with sheets and ropes, clotheslines and blankets, I said, "Just toss it all in the hall."

He did, then came back and sat beside me, gazing at me with mute sympathy. I felt the way you do just before you throw up, weak and sweaty and depressed and kind of gray inside and out. My throat was so dry I couldn't summon the spit to swallow.

The front door opened and Fauncine came in carrying an overnight bag. "Iris, your car's gone."

"Her aunt took it," Byron told her.

Fauncine set her bag on the floor. "She knows?"

"She knows," he said.

"Everything?"

He nodded.

She sat on the other side of me. "Look, Iris, if you feel as if you're really losing it, just signal, and I'll get my dad over here. Trust me. If he starts to get judgmental, I'll remind him of the Hippocratic oath or something."

I remembered Judson Woodridge in the hospital, after he'd set and pinned and plated the bones I'd broken in the ski accident, sitting by my bed, holding my hand. I was groggy then, and scared, and I hurt.

"The trick in living through anything," he said, "is in getting through the next hour."

Byron took my hands between his great grubby paws now. "Try to breathe deep and slow."

He was a lot like Judson Woodridge in a crisis—calm and not intrusive and just *there,* so you felt that he'd be there as long as you needed him.

Staunch was the word that came to my mind. Maybe he wouldn't know a Huguenot from a Fluffy Donut, but he was staunch. "The trick," I said, my voice coming from someplace far above me, "the trick is in living through the next hour."

"Well, I . . ." Fauncine looked at the two of us. "Where are Pete and Alvin?"

"Out back with Foster," Byron told her.

"I'll see if he needs any help," she said, and left us.

Byron put his arm around my shoulder. "We'll figure something out. Listen, when I was younger, I did some things that were so stupid, it scares me even today to think about them. It hurts, but you learn, and if you have any sense, you don't make the same mistakes again."

I drew back a little only so I could look at his face.

"You make new ones," he said.

I would not have believed I'd be able to smile.

"Anyway," he went on, "all those times I thought I'd brought the world down around my ears were awful. But you remember how bad some things were, and you take heart just knowing you survived them."

I was listening to his voice, not just his words but the low, comforting rumble, when Zelma walked in the front door with my aunt.

"We met just now," Zelma said.

"I took it to the body shop near Xiang Lo's." Blanche looked grim. "They just took a quick look, but we're talking hundreds."

Byron stood and helped her to the sofa.

Fauncine came in from the yard carrying Alvin, who looked as if he'd been eating dirt. Foster was with her, hauling Pete, who seemed to have rolled in mud.

I felt like the guest of honor at a wake.

"I think I should tell you that it wasn't Iris's fault at all," Zelma ventured. "I am not taking any legal responsibility, mind you. But if I hadn't kind of . . . encountered her foot, she would have come home with Foster and the car just as it was."

"I know a pretty good auto wrecker," Byron told my aunt. "I can scout around there right away and pick up stuff for a song. And I can do the work for nothing."

"I'll have fifty dollars," I reminded my aunt.

"Eighty," Zelma said. "You can owe me."

"I wonder if you'd leave me alone with my niece for just a few minutes," Blanche said.

They all went quietly through the kitchen to the backyard, not even stopping to wash Pete and Alvin.

The next thing I knew, I was snuffling all over her. "Eighty dollars won't even be . . . begin . . ."

Blanche stroked my hair. "Come on, now. Pull yourself together. We'll let that great gorgeous blond pick up what he can from the wrecker, and we'll trust him with whatever labor you can supervise. I can get an advance on my credit card."

I sat up. "It's going to cost a fortune!"

"Only goodwill comes cheap anymore."

"How will I pay you back?" I cried.

"Oh, you'll be washing my windows and mowing my lawns well into middle age."

I didn't pull myself together for a minute. Nestled there against her, I remembered when I was really little, and she used to rock me and sing me "Who Threw the Overalls in Mrs. Murphy's Chowder?" and show me how she could move the cartilage in her nose from side to side.

I was about to tell her that I had something more remunerative than window washing in the works, but since it would involve Zelma and the use of my mother's car, I thought this might not be the time to bring it up.

"We're not going to lie to your mother, Iris." Blanche was firm.

"Never. Never," I said.

"But there's no use bringing up something that will take all the sparkle out of her vacation. If she found out that you got into such trouble when she went away, she'd never forgive herself. Or me. If she does find out, it will be after the car's fixed. Seeing it now is a good ninety percent of the shock. Could you stop snuffling all over my chest?"

I sat up. "I just . . . I love you, Aunt Blanche. I love you even smelling like the Gilroy Garlic Festival."

"Lunch. I clean forgot. I suppose after the way they rallied around, we should feed your pack. We could order pizza . . . Oh. Sorry. So how about Chinese takeout? I'll bring that strapping blond boy with me in case the car breaks down."

I lifted my head. "Take Foster."

She brushed at her collar. "I never dreamed you had a wild streak in you, Iris. Nothing as wild as I was at your age, but . . ." She looked down at me. "I am bailing you out on a one-time-only basis. You ever pull a string of dumb tricks like this again, you're on your own."

"Not dumb," I protested. "Monumentally dumb."

"You're fifteen. You're entitled."

The day was getting warmer already, and I knew I should shut the windows and the curtains against the afternoon heat, but I needed to stay like this with my aunt a little longer. We sat there for a few more minutes, and then I asked her something that had been lurking in my mind for so many years. "Does it really disappoint you and my mother that I'm not more like Ellie?"

She put her hand under my chin so she could look into my eyes. "Is that what you think?"

"Well, this 'cup of life' stuff. I'm a hotshot athlete, auto mechanic, straight-A student because I *love* all that stuff . . . and poetry and philosophy . . ."

"Oh, Iris." With her sleeve, she wiped my face almost dry. "I think . . . I think your mother and I screwed up if we've pressured you to be any different. I don't know. I'm afraid one generation always has an *agenda* for the next."

"Agenda," I said. "Almost everybody from my first coach on has had an agenda for me."

"And you're entitled to create your own."

"Absolutely. Of course, I'm still figuring it out."

"I'll go for that." She stood. "Just don't think it means you have carte blanche."

I could hear my friends outside.

"Hey, Foster!" I yelled. "You want to cart Blanche to the takeout?"

"One thing I can't stand is a smart-mouth kid," she said.

With Foster cornered at last, Zelma was not about to let him escape. She went with him and my aunt.

Byron and Fauncine took Ellie's boys into the bathroom and cleaned them up for lunch. When they came back into the parlor, she said, "I'm going to take Pete and Alvin for a little walk around the block. You can keep Iris company, Byron."

I wondered if Woodridge had any idea what a great kid he had.

When they'd left us, Byron sat on the sofa beside me again. "You're really going to go into—what kind of business?—with Zelma?" Byron asked.

"Kind of like errands. You know. With Fauncine's brains and Zelma's . . ."

"Audacity."

I grinned. "Well, she's forceful. Foster thinks so."

"They were made for each other."

You can't expect a Viking god to have infallible insight.

"He's been trying to dodge her until he can pay her back," Byron said. "He's crazy about her, and she drives him crazy. It's like being in love with your Nemesis."

Nemesis? Be cool, I told myself. Sure, there's a lot more to him than beauty and brawn. Sure, it was touching that this great, towering male could have a grasp of human relationships. And he was far more interesting than one might have suspected. But *Nemesis?* Of course, there is no law that a biker can't pick up scraps of mythology. He may merely have had good schools and strong-minded teachers.

Still, I took a risk. "So did your parents name you after the poet?"

"I think it was after David Bowie's Screaming Lord Byron. But George Gordon, all the Romantic poets—Keats, Shelley, Byron, Swinburne—were as wild as any rockers. People tend to think of all the nineteenth-century poets as somehow . . . Victorian. But they were out on the edge. When the woman Rossetti loved died . . ."

Had I been Victorian, I might have pressed a hand over my fluttering heart. "Of course, Rossetti was a Pre-Raphaelite," I murmured.

He nodded. "But he ran with the Romantics. When Elizabeth Siddal died, he buried the manuscripts of his poems with her."

"He dug them up again later." You can't let romanticism degenerate into sentimentality.

Byron looked at me the way I would have dreamed he'd look at me, had I not given up on men. "Not many people today know about that. You like poetry."

What the hell, I thought. "Also philosophy."

Byron moved a little closer. "You read Wallace Stevens?"

"Oh, *yeah.*"

"And he was an insurance man," he mused. "So much for making quick judgments about people."

We stared at each other. No. Just as in Keats, we look'd at each other with wild surmise.

And I knew. I was absolutely sure. "Byron, you don't just read poetry. You write it."

He looked down at his football-player hands. He'd scrubbed them almost raw. "Sometimes."

"What a screwed-up time," I said, "when writing poetry is something you *confess* to. If Hemingway's generation was lost, ours is . . ."

". . . severed clean at the roots. I'm pretty good at being part of my generation. You know, broke a few bones in football, look as badass as I have to. But it's living like a double agent. You can't even explain to your best friend that what matters is getting an idea of who you are and what really means anything."

I nodded. "And what is, in the long run, worth doing. But you're right. Especially if you're big and male, you must feel as if you're living in alien territory."

I thought of the song from *Mad Max Beyond Thunderdome* about the children, the last generation. Our generation was, indeed, the one they left behind, left with only shopping malls, talk shows, and tabloid news, and no ties at all to the struggle for a culture, the long, uneven climb to being decent animals.

I almost told Byron that Zelma wrote poetry. She was my friend. She and I had been through a lot together. We might well go into business together. But when you find a man who respects you for your mind and your character, and, just as important, a man you respect for the same . . .

You take me for a fool?

Besides, Foster Prizer *needed* Zelma.

"So, Byron," I said. "Since we're going to be spending some time together over my mother's car, you want to take in a museum after my foot's healed . . . or maybe a track meet?"

He smiled. "I'll bring some of my poems over, too. You remember what happened to Elizabeth

Barrett when she first read Robert Browning's poetry?"

She fell in love with him, sight unseen, but I wasn't going to talk about that yet. There was plenty of time.